THE MONSTERS WITHIN

S. J. SERIO

INFINITE WORLDS, LLC

First Edition May, 2023

Edited by Kerry Stapley and Chelsea Cambeis (Blue Pen – http://www.bluepenbooks.com)

Cover Design created by rebeccacovers

Maps created by BMR Williams

ISBN 979-8-9879112-0-4 (Hardback Edition)

ISBN 979-8-9879112-1-1 (eBook Edition)

ISBN 979-8-9879112-2-8 (Paperback Edition)

Library of Congress Control Number 2023904977

Published by Infinite Worlds, LLC

Publisher Website https://www.infiniteworldspub.com

Author Website https://sjserio.com

Dedicated to Savannah, Sophia, and Lexy.

Thank you for your patience with me.

CONTENTS

Preface	VII
Map	XI
Prologue	XIII
1. At the Office	1
2. Jenna-Bear	11
3. Interrogation	17
4. Celebration	25
5. Encounters	31
6. Hope and Sorrow	37
7. Evening at Home	43
8. Questions	49
9. Containment	55
10. Voices of Children	63
11. The UGC and Me	71
12. The Maze	79
13. Blood on the Floor	87
14. Extra Rations	93

15. The Facility   99

16. The Black Door   107

17. Horrors Unleashed   111

18. The Undercity   121

19. The Cleaners   127

20. Memories and Meetings   135

21. Welcomed News   141

22. The Testing   145

23. The Railbus   153

24. The Wildlands   163

25. A Reprieve   171

26. Carnage   177

27. The Final Run   183

Epilogue   191

Acknowledgments   199

About Author   201

PREFACE

Late January was the beginning of the 2019 spring semester at Towson University. It was my fourth semester there (not counting the summer sessions I had taken). While my major was Social Sciences, the class I was most excited about was Writing Fiction. I had longed to be a writer. You may ask why I didn't major in English or Creative Writing. Well, I love fantasy and science fiction and I considered social sciences would play a big part in worldbuilding. Plus, I figured it would be a good backup program should my writing career fail. The class was interesting from the start. We did our introductions, and the Professor led us to generate a list of genres on the board. He also passed around a sign-up list. The list was for the dates when our first assignment would be due (with the class assessing and critiquing it on the next day). By the time the list made it around to me, the only dates left were the first slots. Those were only two weeks away.

In our first hour together, the professor asked us a couple of polling questions (the nature of which; I forget). For each question, he tallied the hands raised, then counted down the list of genres. The assignment was then settled. We had to write a short story in the genre of "Utopian (/dystopian) Horror."

So it was that I had two weeks to write this story in a genre I had never really explored. Fortunately, my mind was turning right away. I jotted down some notes. When I got home, I began expanding those notes and building the world that I would set my story in. It wasn't long before I had an outline and began writing the story.

On the day of my critique, I was nervous and excited. I had little time to develop this story, but I felt I did a good job, considering. But now was time for my work, "The Monsters Within," to be judged by not only the professor, but my peers as well. Being a creative work, this was more important to me than any term paper I had written.

Fortunately, the critique went well. There were some excellent suggestions for improvement. However, the best compliment I received was from the professor (and echoed by some of my classmates) on how much world building I could accomplish in so little time. This was the encouragement I needed.

I submitted two more stories to the class during the semester, one a "Fantasy Mystery" and the other a "Comedy Western." For my final project, I chose my Utopian Horror to submit as a rewrite (from the critique). I really enjoyed that class.

Sadly, that was my last semester in college. My funding (in the form of the Montgomery GI Bill) ran out, and that spring saw me dealing with the death of somebody close to me. I spent the summer trying to find a job. My daughter was turning four, and I needed something. At the same time, a bug hit me. I published a short story that I had written previously on Kindle and reexamined "The Monsters Within."

I expanded the outline to novella length and began working on a few chapters. Then... I got a job. I shelved the project as I had little time available to write. My priority was providing for my family. Fast forward a few months into the next year and, well, we all know what happened then.

The Great Pandemic of 2020 really gave me pause. The whole catalyst for my story was that a plague caused great upheaval in the world and led to society being how it was. I questioned whether I should go further with it. Also, by this time, I was working at a hospital, so I didn't really have the free time that many others had, so my writing was on pause. In the end, I decided to finish what I had. The outline was already done and much of the book was already written. In the summer of 2021, I returned to the book. After looking at what I had, I decided that the best thing to do was to write it over. I used what I had already written as a guide, changing where I saw it was needed, filling in where I had to, and by the end of August, my first draft manuscript was complete. I placed it in beta read status, invited some readers (both familiar and strangers) and life happened again.

In October 2021, my second daughter was born. I completed some revisions from the beta readers. But between my daughter's birth, plus the holidays, very little progress was made. After the new year, I picked back up again, making plans for the final stages of my book's development.

After several editing sessions, the novella expanded to a full (albeit short) novel. It has been a journey. From taking a short story I wrote for a class assignment to crafting a full novel, I enjoyed every aspect. And now, I share it with you. I hope you enjoy this story.

-S.J. Serio

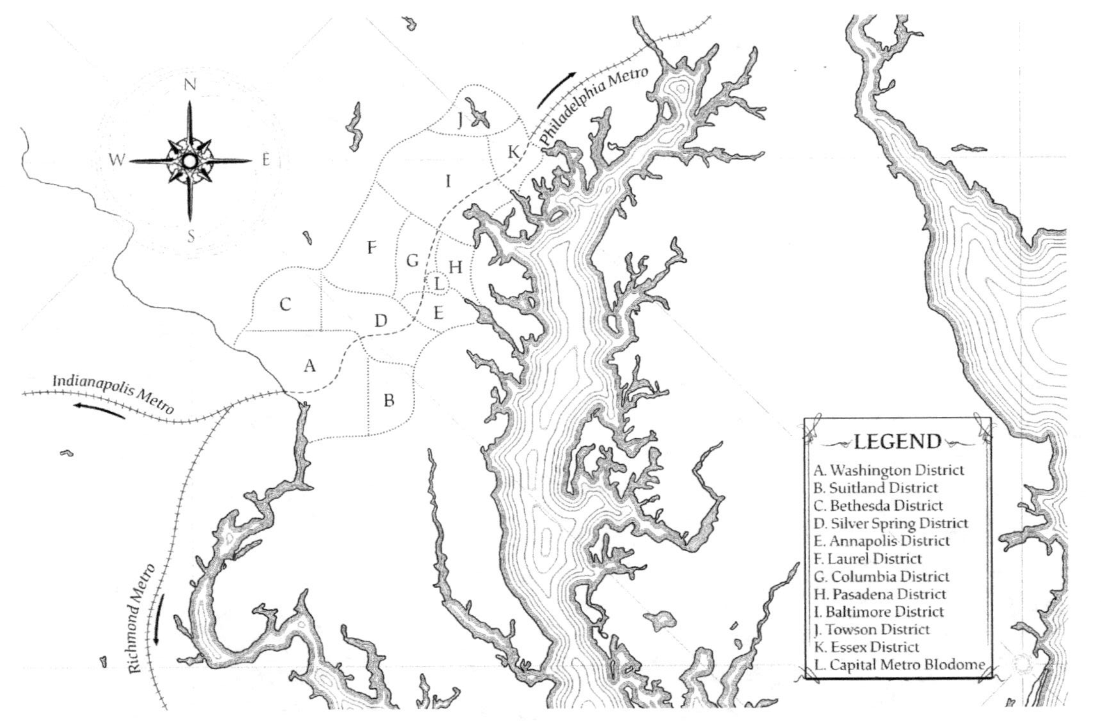

Philadelphia Metro
Indianapolis Metro
Richmond Metro
N
W
E
S
J
K
I
F
G
H
C
L
D
E
A
B
LEGEND
A. Washington District
B. Suitland District
C. Bethesda District
D. Silver Spring District
E. Annapolis District
F. Laurel District
G. Columbia District
H. Pasadena District
I. Baltimore District
J. Towson District
K. Essex District
L. Capital Metro Blodome

PROLOGUE
2163.05.14 | 23:40

Jordan stared at the ceiling. The shadows projected by the scant moonlight penetrating the boarded windows told him it couldn't have been more than a couple of hours since he went to sleep. He could hear the excited shouts coming from the other occupants of the long-abandoned manor house. Any minute now, Chris Edwards would be by to wake him up and get him moving. This was going to be a long night.

It had already been a minute or two since he woke up. What stirred him was the sound of a transport passing over the manor, a TC-10 by the sound of it. He heard the unmistakable sound of the engine as it passed just outside the partially boarded window. He sat up as he heard the inevitable footsteps approaching his door. Raising his hand to his head, he shook the tiredness away and motivated himself to grab his gear and get ready. Just as he pulled his pants up, the door crashed open as Chris Edwards peeked in. The light from the room beyond obscured his features, but Jordan knew it was him from his silhouette. Edwards took one look at him and nodded. "Good, you're already awake."

Jordan pulled his shirt on. "Of course I am! How could anybody sleep with all that noise downstairs?"

Edwards shook his head. "They're up to something. Another transport just flew by. It landed not far from here."

"And Kevin wants me to check it out." He continued putting on his gear, which fit him comfortably. Many operatives wore something similar. The aramid fabrics allowed some protection while maintaining maneuverability. "Tell him I'll be right down."

After Edwards left, Jordan checked his utility belt to make sure he had all his essentials. Then he checked his magna pistol. He preferred the old-fashioned gunpowder-based guns, but these newer weapons often proved a blessing. Their only drawback was that the shots charged. The longer they charged, the more effective they were. But their accuracy was unmatched by the old conventional weapons. When he was satisfied, he buckled the pistol on and walked out the door.

He had to shield his eyes as he entered the hallway. They had not yet adjusted. Normally, the lights would be off to preserve energy and minimize the risk of being discovered. Not that the latter was an enormous risk. The United Global Coalition rarely came out into the Wildlands. Still, it was better to be safe.

Jordan walked down the stairs. When he reached the main room of the old manor house, Edwards was waiting by the foyer entrance, ready to go. Kevin stood by a table, looking over a map. The only light in the room shone down on it. Though he was close in height to Jordan, the others constantly hazed Kevin about his short stature. His light brown hair, which normally draped to his shoulders, was now tied back in a ponytail. The light cast eerie shadows on Kevin that made his already bronze skin appear darker, almost as dark as Jordan.

A couple of operatives, a man and a woman whose names he had not quite learned yet, were also in the room. The woman, her sandy blonde hair also in a ponytail, had just entered carrying some papers and books that she put on the table before heading back out. The man was by a window, peering through the boards at the darkness. Jordan approached the table and looked at the map. It was from a time before the great urban migration, when there was still life here, and detailed the area surrounding the manor house. "What do we have?"

Kevin, who was deeply focused on the map, didn't even flinch at Jordan's voice. Still looking at the map, he responded, "Judging by the direction of the craft and its speed, this is the likely location." He placed his finger on the map, indicating a clearing about two kilometers from the manor. Jordan studied the area for a moment. He knew it well. He thought about where he could get the best vantage point for observation of any activities in that clearing.

"All right, then... Let's get this done." He started toward Edwards, but Kevin grabbed his arm as he passed.

Kevin was looking at him intently now. "Be extra careful. There have been strange reports."

"Reports of what?"

"It is uncertain. Nobody has gotten close enough to determine what is going on at those sites, but after the landings, strange screams have been heard in the wilderness, and animals have been found mutilated. Whatever is going on..." He left the thought hanging.

Finally, he released his grip on Jordan's arm. Jordan assured him with a nod and moved on to Edwards. "Let's go!" he said as he walked through the door.

The two men left the manor and went down to the road in front. Jordan stopped and looked around, his eyes adjusting to the night. He got his bearings and started toward the clearing.

They hadn't gotten too far when Edwards broke the silence of their march. "This is the third one in the past twenty-four hours. I've heard the UGCs have been making these trips for the past week now. The first one was up near old York."

Jordan considered that. He had heard the same. They appeared to be dropping something off. Very little details had made it around besides that. Most of the points had been too far to investigate. Whatever the UGC was up to, it wasn't good.

Edwards was still talking, though Jordan had missed most of what he said. It seemed like he had shifted to the topic of their outpost at the manor house. He was going on about the woman and how "fine" she looked and how he couldn't wait to get to know her better. That was Edwards. He was slick as oil and loved a good time. But he knew how to get the job done. The two of them had just reported to the manor the prior day. They started working together three years ago when Jordan arrived at the principal base in the Appalachians to the west, near Winchester. Jordan was the scout. He was good at learning terrain and could quickly assess any situation.

Back at the base, people lightheartedly teased Edwards, saying that he should have been the scout, given his heritage. Before the Great Plague, Edwards's family lived on a reservation out west. After the Plague, they escaped to Kansas City Metro and lived up to the standards of the UGC until his father was exiled into the Wildlands. Chris may not have made a good scout, but he was otherwise a good jack-of-all-trades. He had a ton of useful talents, not least of which was his ability to drive or pilot any vehicle. He was a good backup to have. Chris Edwards had pulled Jordan's hair out of the fire a few times when things got too heated.

Most of their operations took them around Capital Metro, but some were as far north as New York Metro. They had become well known in the outsider settlements, communities of people exiled from the UGC, some as far back as the Great Plague. York was one of those communities.

Jordan noted that Edwards had stopped talking. They were nearing the clearing. Jordan stopped to get the lay of the land. Much of this region had been farmland before the pandemic and subsequent migration to the cities. With the absence of people, it didn't take long for the area to fill in as the wilderness took over. Jordan knew this place; he was raised here. Lights sparkled through the trees and foliage bordering the clearing.

He turned to Edwards. "Stay here!"

Edwards acknowledged with a nod and found a place to shelter behind some bushes.

Jordan approached the clearing and sought the tallest, sturdiest tree. He pulled a cord from his belt. It had a weighted end, which he cast up to a decent-sized branch about midway up. Using the cord, he quickly climbed the tree to the branch and perched there, looking out over the clearing. He could see several UGC officials moving about. They had unloaded ten large crates. Jordan accessed another pouch on his belt and retrieved a set of digital binoculars. He held them up for a better view, then pressed a button to record. He saw that there were several guards with charge-guns patrolling around the crates. Two more were on top of the crates, attaching lines to pins. Grated holes in the crates showed there must have been something living in those crates...something wild. When they were done, the guards on top gave a signal, and they all headed back into the transport craft.

In a matter of seconds, the craft lifted off. The tether lines attached to the pins tightened as the craft moved. Nearly in unison, the lines pulled the pins out of the crates. From the jerking of the pins being removed, the planks where the pins were attached fell over, leaving the crates wide open. The lines rapidly retracted to the craft as it left the site. With the craft gone, Jordan's binoculars switched to night vision mode. There was a slight delay as they adjusted.

Two of the crates were open at the ends, facing Jordan. He was shocked by the contents. A single person occupied each crate. *Why were they separated?* he wondered. He zoomed in for a better look. The people seemed hesitant to leave their crates. Of the two that Jordan could see, one was a woman, the other a man. They were naked. He noticed movement from the other crates. Some of the mysterious people cautiously emerged. He could see a range of people, from older to young, perhaps as young as teenagers. There was something odd about them—the way they moved, the way they looked. Jordan felt unnerved.

Their heads jerked oddly as something caught their attention near the edge of the clearing. Jordan scanned in the direction of the disturbance. A deer slowly entered from the thicket. Its caution gave way to curiosity at the newcomers. He observed the people and noticed something strange. They were tensing their bodies as a predator tensed before striking its prey. Without warning, the clearing came alive with movement, leaving Jordan struggling to keep track. The people pounced on the deer.

Jordan cursed aloud, a mistake that he never made. The people turned to face his direction despite the distance. It was over; he had to get out of there. Without hesitation, he leaped down from his perch and rolled to a run. Passing by Edwards, he yelled a warning to run, but didn't stop in his stride.

As he ran, Jordan thought about what struck him as odd about the people. There was a wildness to them, a feral demeanor. These were not people, not anymore. They were beasts. He could hear footsteps behind him and only hoped that it was Edwards. How quickly they'd descended on the deer was all too fresh in his mind.

The manor house was in view now; Jordan pushed hard to reach the steps. He dared a glance back and saw Edwards about twenty paces behind. To his dismay, several of the beasts were hot on their trail.

Jordan reached the stairs and rushed up to the porch of the manor. He swung around and grabbed his pistol from the holster on his belt. At the same time, the door to the manor house opened, and Kevin and the other two operatives came out with rifles.

"What the hell?" someone exclaimed as they all lined up along the rail. Edwards was feeling the heat as several of the beasts were on his heels. Jordan took the first shot and hit one square in the chest. It barely fazed the creature. A shot blasted out of one of the rifles and nailed one dead center. It stumbled but kept on running. Another bolt struck the same one, and it collapsed to the ground.

One down out of the five that pursued. It didn't matter to Edwards, though. He stumbled as he ran, and that gave the closest creature the edge it needed. It struck him with a clawed hand. The force sent him rolling forward, blood spraying from an opened artery.

Everything was happening so fast.

Kevin called for a retreat. The other two ran back into the manor house as Kevin grabbed Jordan and dragged him into the manor. The female operative closed the door, bolting it shut. Kevin put Jordan against the wall in the foyer. Jordan could hear agonizing screams coming from outside. Then they cut off. His partner for the past three years was dead. It was all so sudden.

"What the hell were those things?" Kevin's voice sounded hollow.

Jordan mustered a reply. "It was what they dropped off in the clearing. They were in crates and released as the craft left the scene."

Kevin turned to one operative. "Go to the comm station. Get out a signal at once."

"We have been ordered to maintain silence," said the male operative.

"Does it look like I give a shit? Do it!"

The man rushed out at Kevin's order. Jordan looked at the door. Thuds and scratches filled the foyer. Through a small window, he could see an eye peering in at them. It was so human looking, yet so wild. A crash sounded from somewhere in the manor. Suddenly, the pounding at the door stopped.

"Shit!" shouted the other operative as she readied her rifle. Jordan raised his pistol as time seemed to freeze.

There was a rush of footsteps. "I got the message a—" The man's voice ended in a gurgle.

Movement at the entrance of the main hall triggered a reflex shot from the female operative. A bolt of energy blasted past and hit the already lifeless body of the male operative. Just behind it, one creature came rushing in. Jordan fired a shot that struck its head. It fell back and twitched for a moment as another creature came in right behind. Kevin raised his rifle just as the creature bore down on him. Jordan watched as it ripped Kevin's arm off, along with the rifle, and threw it aside.

The beast that Jordan shot staggered upright. It wasn't dead. It didn't matter. Another beast was rushing behind as the first one turned its attention to the woman. She switched her rifle to quick-shot mode that allowed her to shoot multiple bolts with less energy in rapid succession. It had little effect, as the monster overcame the rifle quickly and fell atop her.

Her screams filled the foyer as the other beast lunged into Jordan. He slammed against the wall and slumped to the floor as the beast began tearing at him. At that moment, he realized he was clutching something with his left hand. It was his binoculars. He realized he had never stopped the recording. It was a slight comfort that somebody would see what happened here. They would arrive at the scene and recover the recording and know what they were up against. It also occurred to him he could not feel the pain of the beast tearing his flesh from his bones anymore. That was his last thought before blackness swallowed him whole.

CHAPTER ONE

AT THE OFFICE

2163.05.17 | 10:04

Brett sat back in his chair, giving his eyes and hands a brief rest. He had already been there for a couple of hours comparing the data he was assigned to what was in the database. He made corrections as needed, added information, and noted discrepancies. The simplicity of the job balanced the monotony. He liked that. All he had to do was what was assigned to him. Very little responsibility weighed on his shoulders. For six hours a day, six days a week, this was his life. It wasn't a prestigious job, but it was what he knew…what he was trained to do.

A glance at the wall of the office building revealed that the time was now 10:04 in the morning. Normally, he would have four hours remaining in his work shift; however, today was a special day. The office was closing at noon. Today was the Centennial Celebration, marking one hundred years since the United Global Coalition, commonly referred to as the UGC, saved the world from the Great Plague of the twenty-first century. At 14:00, they planned a grand celebration at the Old National Mall in the Capital District. The Regional President of North America was set to give a speech, and there would be special rations handed out to the attendees.

Brett took a breath and rubbed his face to shake loose the strain from staring at the monitor. Then he ran his hand through his dark brown hair before leaning forward, regaining his focus. He just had to get through a couple more hours. Meticulously, he continued working on today's assignment to input and verify data from the Bureau of Citizens into the UGC master database. The information from the Bureau provided updates to the details of every citizen in the city. It was important to have trained eyes on this data to ensure that the database was accurate and up to date. That information included everything from the basic details of a citizen, such as their birth date and physical description, their occupation, and their current status. Most of the updates were minute illnesses or incapacities, marriages, births, or deaths. Also included were the citizens' daily activities as recorded by city surveillance, check-ins, and incident reports.

Tempting as it was for Brett to look up his own details, he knew that such an act would be a violation. Access to records was tracked, and the punishment was extreme. The system was set up so that nobody would be assigned data that correlated to themselves or any of their relatives or close friends. This was for protection and to stop anybody from altering their own information. In fact, another office handled any information or updates for anybody in the Annapolis District office. Should any such data slip through, it was to be reported immediately to the supervisor.

Brett went over the data on his tablet and pulled up the records. His fingers glided over the screen. He stopped immediately as he stared at the data before him. His eyes went back and forth from the data to the record as he tried to sort it out. Something was troubling him.

Brett leaned in. The record was for a citizen named "John Lewis." There were many holes in his record, and it listed his status as "Deceased" with a date of death as "2161-0812." However, the form entry that Brett pulled up was dated "2163-0425" and listed John Lewis's status as "Contained." This was the third such discrepancy that Brett had come across this morning. The first was a man named "Joseph Lawrence," who was listed deceased as of five years ago but had a form entry that listed him as "Unknown" just last month. Another listed a woman named "Alice Jacobson," whose record showed her as "Retired" this year, but the form listed a death date of "2156-1113."

Brett noted the discrepancies and tapped his tablet to the monitor to transfer the notations and logs. He had sent the first two over for supervisor review. He knew it would be examined, eventually. However, "once is happenstance, twice a coincidence, and three times a conspiracy," as his father had once told him. Brett knew he had to bring this to his supervisor's immediate attention.

He locked his workstation and picked up the tablet. As he stood, he peered around the room. His eyes scanned over the security bot that seemed alerted to his sudden movement as he navigated the maze of cubicles. Its single eye was glowing red as a warning that all employees needed to remain in the office. He reached the door to his supervisor's office and knocked.

"Enter!" came the woman's voice. The name on the office door read "Stacy Houston."

Brett entered the room and stood before the desk. "Mrs. Houston, I have something that I thought I should bring to your immediate attention."

His supervisor looked up from her terminal and regarded him. She was about ten years older than him; he knew. She kept her hair in a bun, as was customary, especially in a business environment. It was lighter than his, but her skin was slightly darker.

He handed her the tablet and continued. "There are several records that I came across in the last hour that have some discrepancies. Some list the respective citizen as deceased, in some cases for several years. However, the new records give other information. I already flagged the first two I came across for further review, but with the growing number of records that I encountered, I thought I should bring them to you immediately."

Mrs. Houston looked over the information. As he explained the discrepancies, she nodded in confirmation. Brett stood there patiently, waiting for her to respond.

Finally, she looked up and smiled. "Thank you, Mr. Hardin, for bringing this to me. This does seem strange. I will have the administrators investigate this immediately." She looked at the clock and back at Brett. "Even though today is a short day due to the Centennial, I think you have earned yourself a break. Go ahead and take it. You have twenty minutes."

Brett thanked her and left the office. Not wanting to waste any of his time, he went immediately to the break room. Walking in, he noticed that one of his coworkers, Eric Larson, was sitting at the table watching the newscast. It was odd for Brett to find him there. But Brett's own time was limited, and he didn't want to waste it worrying about the likes of Eric.

A glance at the screen confirmed what Brett had already suspected—the news talk would be about nothing other than the coming celebration, Brett walked over to the refreshment station and pulled out a cup, placed it in the fountain dispenser, and let it fill with water.

Once the cup was filled, Brett took it, walked over to the table, sat down, and lost himself in the newscast. Presently, they were going over the history of the last 112 years since the Plague gripped the world. It started in rural areas. At first, it affected crops, spoiling the food at rapid rates. This soon led to a famine in parts of the world, while richer countries started seeing an exodus from rural areas to the metropolitan regions.

Then, the Plague mutated.

People were being affected. They would become feverishly sick, turning pale, almost a grayish color. Once it took hold, those that survived were left a husk of their former selves. Most victims, however, succumbed to death. It was at this point that the nations of the world came together and formed a coalition that would handle the global disaster, the UGC.

The response was immediate. The great metros set up large camps on the outskirts where the refugees from the country would be kept in quarantine. Vast projects were started to handle the growth in urban populations. Walls were built to surround major metros so that no one could bypass the checkpoints and make their way into the cities. Each of the metros constructed massive bio-domes where they would grow food, unaffected by the Plague, which could feed the populace. Work also began on infrastructure, raising most of the cities off ground level with a massive network of magnetic monorails intertwining and connecting the major metro areas. The once open spaces, such as parks or forests, were filled in with apartments to handle the growing population.

The broadcast continued its history lesson, speaking of the first metros to be completed. These were the major cities across the world. London, Rome, Paris, and Berlin were among the first in Europe. Tokyo, Beijing, and Hong Kong in Asia. Sadly, some of the lesser developed nations disappeared completely. In America, cities like New York and Los Angeles were among the first to be completed, along with this city where Brett lived and worked.

Now known as Capital Metro, it was a large area. Originally, the metros of Washington, Baltimore and Annapolis were separate. But within decades, the area in between was filled with residential blocks that merged the three metros into one. The broadcast showed a map of Capital Metro and the districts. Stretching from the Potomac River to the Chesapeake Bay and north past Baltimore District, Capital Metro was the largest Metro in the world. It became the center of the North American Region of the UGC.

"It's amazing how something so small, so microscopic, can wreak such havoc and cause drastic change as to reform society in the blink of an eye."

Brett pulled his mind back to the present and blinked at the statement. He looked at the speaker, his coworker. He got so lost in the telecast that he forgot Eric was there. "Excuse me?"

Eric just laughed. "It doesn't matter. We don't really matter. We are all just the cogs of this society, turning the wheels that spin the Earth."

Brett was confused. As he tried to sort out the strange comment, he took a deeper look at his coworker. His sandy blond hair looked as if somebody mussed it, and stubble dotted his face. His work shirt wasn't fastened straight and appeared a bit wrinkly. It was a wonder the man was even there. Brett wondered why Eric was sitting in the break room and not at his terminal, or on disciplinary hold? Brett spoke to break the awkwardness. "Did something happen to you?"

Eric turned to him; his face serious. "Yes! You could say that. It doesn't matter, anyway. Hey...you have a daughter, right? Isn't she about to turn five?"

The sudden change in topic jarred Brett. "Yes, she is." He had never been that close to Eric. Of course, fraternizing of any sort was frowned upon. Though some did, to an extent, they often kept it quiet. Brett refrained from doing so. He had his own life to worry about. "Her birthday is next week. She is scheduled for her evaluation."

Eric continued to stare at Brett, his eyes intense. "Do yourself a favor. Don't take her."

Brett was confused. "That's impossible. You know it is mandatory."

"Listen to me! If you want what is best, you will take her away. Far away! Don't let the UGC get their claws in her. Take your family and just leave."

The suggestion horrified Brett. "What? That... I couldn't! Where would I even take her?"

"To the Wildlands," Eric replied without hesitation. "It's safer there. Much safer."

Brett shook his head. "That would be madness. You are mad. What happened to you? To even suggest such a thing is..."

Eric's laughter interrupted Brett. "Madness! That's right; you are a faithful loyalist. You do whatever you are told by the UGC. Mark my words—it will rip you apart. They will eat you alive." Eric stared at Brett intently, his face distorting to disgust. "You don't even realize how lucky you are."

Brett stared back at the man. He was clearly unhinged. Footsteps echoed from outside the breakroom and three people entered. Stacy Houston, flanked by two others in PPU uniforms, regarded the pair. Stacy turned toward Brett. "Mr. Hardin! Your break is almost over. It is time for you to return to your station."

Brett jumped from his seat. He nodded and quickly headed out of the room. As he left, he heard Eric chuckling. He reached his station and sat down, barely in time. As he logged on and resumed his work, a commotion rang out through the office—a thud followed by a succession of zaps. Brett reflexively popped up from his cubicle and noticed that his coworkers were doing the same.

A moment later, the two UGC officials came out with Eric in restraints. He looked dazed. Brett realized that the two officials were members of the Protection and Preservation Unit, or PPU. Some jokingly referred to them as "Cleaners." The PPU acted as the police force of the UGC. As they reached the entrance with their prisoner, the eye on the security robot turned green to allow them to pass, then turned red again once they were through. Stacy came out of the break room and looked around. She called everybody's attention.

"There is no need for alarm," she began. "The PPU has removed a threat from our midst. It was discovered that your coworker, Eric Larson, was an agent of the Gray Roses terrorist organization. I know it may be concerning having such a creature among us. However, let me assure you that his vile deeds have been minimized, and any damage that he has done is being corrected as we speak. He is being taken for interrogation and he will NOT resist. As you know, the PPU are experts at extracting information. These deplorable criminals will fail in their nefarious plots against the free peoples of the UGC."

She scanned the room, looking at each person individually, it seemed. Finally, she continued. "With that said, I understand that this is a lot to deal with, having one of your coworkers suddenly escorted out. Knowing that you have worked beside him, maybe had conversations with him, you may feel filthy. I have received authorization to end the workday. Go now and focus on today's magnificent celebration. Put Eric Larson out of your minds and focus on the United Global Coalition and your place within it."

Upon completing her speech, she returned to her office. Brett looked down and saw that his workstation had a green icon, indicating that he was authorized to log out and leave. He did just that and made his way to the door. The bot's eye was now green, and people filed out. He paused as he approached Stacy Houston's office. He turned and knocked, and she welcomed him in.

Before he could say anything, she smiled and said, "You need not worry, Mr. Hardin. You are cleared. Monitors in the breakroom revealed the conversation, and we do not suspect you as an accomplice. We all know that you will not listen to a word that lunatic said and will do your duty to your family, and most importantly, the UGC."

"Th...thank you!" Brett stammered. She had known exactly what he wanted to talk about. He supposed that made sense, given the circumstances.

Mrs. Houston continued. "Are you heading to the Mall for the ceremony?"

"Yes, I'm meeting my family there." The words were slow to come out at first, as he was still shaken by the events that had just unfolded.

"Well now, go! Enjoy the festivities."

Brett nodded and exited the room. He walked past the security bot and pulled out his comm phone. He called Lindsey, his wife, and explained that he was leaving now and that he would meet her and the kids outside the Museum. With that, he made his way to the railbus platform and awaited the next railbus heading toward the inner capital.

Chapter Two

JENNA-BEAR

2163.05.17 | 10:40

The wind found the gaps in her gown and filled it as it flowed across her body. It was a light wind, only slightly more than a breeze, given the height of the balcony. It complemented the mild temperatures of the mid-spring morning. Jenna closed her eyes as the wind caressed her skin under her gown. It felt good for a change.

She had arrived in the city the previous evening. For months she had been in the south undergoing extensive training in the Carolina Wildlands. She had been on missions before, but she was preparing for an important mission that took her to Atlanta Metro. It was a challenging mission, but rewarding both for her and for the Gray Roses. They gained a lot of supplies, particularly weaponry and technology, which would be put to great use. Then she got a short reprieve back in Old Winchester in the mountains to the west, where she got to spend some time with Amanda. It was too brief, however.

Now, she was back in Capital Metro, where her life had begun. At least she was with the other love of her life, though of a different type. Her sister, Kara, was inside the apartment, preparing for a mission of her own. Jenna did not know the details. That fact alone told her it was dangerous. She looked out over the city. The view wasn't much. A forest of apartment buildings stretched out before her. This was one of the older apartment buildings from before the Plague. Other than the fresh air she could get from standing on it, the balcony was otherwise useless.

She heard the balcony door slide open behind her, but did not move. A soft but stern voice she grew up with, only now more mature, broke her thoughts. "You've been standing out here a while."

Jenna turned to regard her sister. Her golden hair, which she inherited from their mother, was tied back in a ponytail, and she wore the standard civilian clothes of UGC citizens: khaki pants and a white shirt with a tan jacket with a flap that stretched across her chest. Whatever her mission, she was going incognito.

"It feels good out here."

Kara raised a brow. "Standing out here with nothing but that shirt on, you will probably get sick."

"It's a nightgown. And it covers me...enough."

"Now Jenna, I know you would stand out here naked if you could get away with it, but if one of the security bots spots you in their scans, it may consider that shirt indecent enough to come investigate."

Jenna gave a sly smile. "They shouldn't make those robots so *pervy!*"

Kara stared back, her expression stern. She couldn't hold it, though, and finally broke out laughing. Jenna laughed, too, and followed her sister into the apartment. It wasn't an enormous apartment, but it was obscure enough that Rachel was able to secure it for them when they were in the city.

Jenna looked at her sister. "You are about ready to go!" she said bluntly.

"I am!" came the blunt response.

Jenna looked away, back toward the balcony. "I wish...I wish I could go with you."

"No, Jenna! You have your tasks and I have mine. You know that. Since we started, Rachel thought it was a good idea that we work separately. I agree with her."

"I know! It's just..." She paused as she felt a tear forming in her eye. "We hardly ever see each other anymore. There is always a job to be done. I barely get to see you...to see Amanda. We are constantly moving. Up and down this forsaken land. And for what?"

"You know the fight! You know why we do this. Remember our father? Remember what he saw? What he died for?"

Jenna slumped at those words. "I do!" Jenna was too young when they died. But she had learned what happened. Their father was a prominent figure in the UGC. He confessed to their mother that he had seen horrible things. He was aligning away from the organization altogether. She understood. She saw how it was wrecking him. Then, one day, their mother took Jenna to pick up Kara from her school. They stopped at the ration depot, and when they returned to their home, their father was hanging in the bedroom.

Jenna vaguely remembered the scene. She was the one who walked in and saw him. When her sister followed, the scream she gave was blood curdling. The cleaners wrote it up as a suicide. But their mother knew otherwise. Eventually, they ended up living in the under city, in some abandoned old ruin of a house. Then, their mother disappeared. Something had happened to her. The two girls were left to survive on their own.

Jenna looked back at Kara. "I miss those days...when you took care of me and told me everything was going to be alright."

Kara looked confused. "What happened? You are not like this. You are one of the toughest girls I know. What is going on?"

"Everything has happened! From Dad's death to our days in the Undercity, to the time that Rachel discovered us, took us in, and started training us for what we have become today. All of it has made me hard. You as well. But don't you ever wish you could just be fragile for a change? That we could just wrap ourselves in the arms of a lover and let all our worries go?"

Kara's face softened. "Jenna, sweetie! I do dream of that moment. When we can be carefree and just live our lives. That day will come. But we do what we must to achieve that dream." She grabbed Jenna's arms and pulled her to face to face with her. Her deep green eyes peered directly into Jenna's. "I promise you that one day, we will be free. That is what we are fighting for." Then Kara pulled Jenna close and squeezed her in a big hug.

Jenna just accepted the embrace. She melted in her sister's arms. "You, me, and Amanda should just leave...go out west. Out to the wide-open stretches far from the UGC's reach."

Kara squeezed her tighter. "You know they will only catch up to us, eventually. No! We must fight. We must tear down this awful structure that is the UGC. Only then can we be truly free."

Finally, Jenna pulled back from the hug and looked her sister in the eyes. Even though her own hair was a medium brown, in sharp contrast to Kara's golden hair, staring at Kara's face was almost like looking into a mirror. "I love you, Kara! You have always been there for me. Like you said, I am a hard person. I know I must be. Even around Amanda and especially around Rachel. But I am glad that I have you where I can be vulnerable for a change."

"Always!" Kara smiled and then released her grasp on Jenna's arms. She turned to grab her bag and started for the door.

"Kara!" She stopped and turned back. "When this is all done, when we finally have a break, promise me you will tell me a story like you did when we were little."

Kara cracked a wide smile at that, her eyes glistening. She shook her head. "I promise, Jenna-bear!" Jenna almost broke at the sound of the name that she hadn't heard since she was a child. The name her father used to call her, and Kara picked up after they were left alone. Kara turned and walked out the door.

Jenna stood there for a time after Kara left. She turned back to the balcony, tempted to go back out and watch her sister leave the building below.

Finally, she went to the bedroom where her bag was. She moved her bag onto the bed, then looked into the nearby mirror. She wiped her face. Her sister was right. They couldn't run. They had to fight. Things were ramping up, and it seemed like this movement was going to explode into something more very soon. She had to be a part of it. Jenna closed her eyes and focused. She could feel the weakness leaving her, her strength filling up the void inside like liquid fire.

She grappled with her emotions, wrestled them down, and pushed them away. When she opened her eyes again, they were like brown flames in her reflection. Gone was that weak child she once was, that she had allowed to return that morning. Now, she was the hardened warrior that her life had forged her to be. She pulled off the gown. Rachel would be waiting to meet her at the celebration.

Digging through her bag, she retrieved her own civilian clothes. How she hated wearing those things. They were like a uniform of indignity. But she would do what she had to do. For Amanda, for Kara, and for herself. She looked back at the mirror as she pulled the slacks on. Oh yes! Those flames were back in her eyes. She was ready to give the UGC hell.

Chapter Three

INTERROGATION

2163.05.17 |12:00

The room was completely black. Eric did not know how long he had been there. After he was taken into custody, he was loaded into a transport with no windows. When he was finally taken out, the transport was inside a hangar from which he was immediately escorted by a couple of Cleaners. Not the ones that arrested him—lower-level guards who brought him to this current room. They fastened him to the lone chair in the center of the room, then left. Just after they did, the lights turned off, leaving him in this total darkness.

At first, he tried to count the minutes. That became futile. So, he sat there, alone in his thoughts. Interesting tactics.

His mind wandered. He reflected on how he got there. The events that led to his capture. From the outset, things had gone wrong. And it all came down to his bloody conscience. Rachel would have never approved of his last assignment. She placed him in that office to monitor the data. It was simple—monitor the records that went into the database, look out for information regarding fellow Gray Roses members, and take any measures to protect them.

He worked years at that task without a hitch. He was well integrated within the office. Nobody suspected a thing. He did his job diligently—not just his task that he was assigned, but his job for the UGC. He had to maintain his cover. And he did it well.

Then came the assignment. He heard rumblings amongst the network that something happened that spooked the Roses' higher-ups. Stories of monsters and mutilations in the Wildlands. The assignment had to come from Mitch. That bastard was the only one that would give such an assignment. Rachel knew better, and that wasn't Joe's style. Mitch, on the other hand, seemed to have some sort of personal vendetta and looked for any opportunity to cause chaos within the UGC.

But Eric was nothing if not dutiful. He had his own gripes against the UGC. So, over the past week, he collected the materials needed and constructed the bomb. They were going to give those idiots a Centennial to remember. He got the bomb into place at the data center. An excellent spot, too.

Of course, he knew it was a suicide mission. His only chance to survive would be to get past the security bots before the bomb went off. But that was nearly impossible. However, that wasn't the reason that he couldn't go through with it. It was those damned fools he spent years working beside.

He pitied them. They went about their days living their lives under the laws and regulations of the UGC. He supposed he couldn't blame them. They were provided homes and food for their entire lives. Well, until they were "retired." Still. For them, all they had to do was their *duty*. Most of them did not understand the concept of freedom. So, they didn't even know what they were missing.

Eric began thinking about that fool in the break room, Brett. Their conversation. The guy had kids. While Eric was not above hurting others for the cause, these people were innocent. The actual monsters were those in the UGC, the Regional President and her cronies. They were the enemy, not these poor schmucks trying to live their lives as best as they could.

Suddenly, the room filled with a brilliant light. It stung his eyes so much that he shut them tight, wincing. He could hear the click of the door and footsteps approaching. Gradually, he opened his eyes.

As his vision adapted, he could see that the entire wall to his left was now gone, or appeared to be. If the view wasn't just a projection, the room he was in appeared to be high, with a clear view of the Capital Mall. He could see the crowd gathering by the structure known as the Washington Monument. It was the most people gathered in one place he had ever seen. Judging from the sunlight, it was afternoon now.

"Enjoying the view?" The speaker was a woman and stood in front of him. He turned to regard her. It was the same woman that took him into custody. She wore charcoal-gray slacks and vest over a solid white shirt. The standard uniform of an agent of the PPU. Eric knew that guards, like the ones who escorted him to this room, wore a dark blue version of the same uniform and grunts wore olive green. Her reddish-brown hair was tied back in a bun, and her skin was on the pale side.

Beside her, her partner wore a similar uniform. He had slightly darker skin and his hair was closely cut. He was perhaps of a more Middle Eastern heritage. Not that any of that mattered in the UGC. They all had Westernized names, at least here in the North American region. The UGC long ago standardized names in their attempt to remove culture from the populace. It made them easier to control. A glance at their badges over their left breasts confirmed their names to be John Evans and Melissa Davis.

The woman stared intently at him. He just gave a smile. "The view is wonderful. I thank you for such wonderful accommodations, though I could do without these restraints."

The woman smiled back. "I am Agent Davis. This is Agent Evans. We will handle your processing during your stay here." Evans pushed a button near the door and a bench folded out from the wall. They sat down on the bench across from Eric and watched him.

He regarded the pair as they stared at him. He knew the drill. They were looking for tells in his posture and expressions. He was well trained, though. "I thank you for joining me. I look forward to a wonderful conversation."

Evans, his face showing no amusement, leaned in. "Mr. Larson. We have your bomb. Crudely made, but it certainly would have caused significant damage and loss of life. The only reason that you are still breathing right now is because you did not detonate it. This is hardly a time for jokes."

Eric met the man's eyes and smirked. "What's the matter, big guy? Did your mommy forget to starch your underwear?"

The agent sat back and even had a smirk of his own. But Eric knew it was not a smile of humor. More like he knew he had the size and likely strength advantage. Eric was getting to him.

"You want conversation," said Davis. "Then let's converse. Tell me, why did you NOT detonate the bomb?"

Eric shrugged. "I don't know. I guess I'm just a softy."

"I think that you never really wanted to set it off to begin with. You've worked at that office for years. You've developed a close bond with your coworkers. You didn't want to hurt them."

The agent never removed her gaze from him the whole time she spoke. She never even blinked. Eric met her eyes just as intently. "Close? What is 'close' in this city? How can anybody get 'close' with anyone? You can't get 'close' to any person you aren't assigned to get 'close' to. That's the way you people want it."

"So why not detonate it?"

"What purpose would it have served?"

"It would have caused great devastation on such an important day." She paused for a moment. "I think that you never liked the idea to begin with. Somebody in your organization wanted it done, and you were opposed."

"What organization might you be referring to?" Eric replied.

Evans interjected, "Cut the crap! We know you are a member of the Gray Roses terrorist group. We've looked over your history. You think that we only just learned of you? We have been watching you for a while. You avoided being assigned a wife. No other family of note. Your father died in an accident when you were a child, and your mother went off to retirement nine years ago, not long before you started working at the data center. Since then, you have been exhibiting odd behavior. Traveling different routes to and from your home. Going to ration depositories in areas out of the way from where you live. You have barely even spent any of your credits."

Eric barely stifled a flinch at the mention of his mother. Instead, he smiled again. "Congratulations. How very astute of you. I'd clap, but...well." He nodded down at the restraints on his hands.

Davis spoke up. "Mr. Larson. Things aren't looking good for you. We will move you to a holding facility later today. It would be in your interest to cooperate with us while you can."

"What would it matter? We both know that my life is forfeited, just like my mother's. Yes! I know how the UGC's *retirement plan* works. I know that my mother has been pushing up daisies since she left for Miami Metro. Only the elite truly get to *retire*. As far as my cooperation goes, you have me. I practically turned myself in."

"Why did you?"

Eric looked at the woman. He didn't know what it was, but he softened a little. "Look! Yeah, I didn't like the order. What was the point? Take out the data center and it would have done little good."

"But you built the bomb, anyway. You planned to do it, even though you were opposed."

"Yeah, so what?" Eric studied the woman for a moment. "There's this old game called chess. Have you ever heard of it?"

The question caught her. It was faint, but Eric saw it. "Yes, I have. Some still play it. I did back in the Academy."

"Then you understand. You have your different pieces, the rooks, the knights, the pawns."

"Yes, I am aware." She was clearly intrigued now.

"You see, you would be a knight. Somebody like Stacy Houston would be a rook. The rest of the schmucks at the office are just pawns. Most of them don't even realize that they are in a game. They just do what they are told. Sent aimlessly forward while the big pieces hold back and protect the king. Those big pieces...they are the ones with the power. They can make special moves that can often carry them across the board. They eat up the pawns without hesitation."

Davis sat for a moment, staring at Eric. "So, why did you turn yourself in, Mr. Larson?"

Eric hesitated before answering. "Because I am no more than a pawn for the other side. For my side. I knew that to follow through was nothing more than a gambit."

Evans spoke up this time. "So, are you saying that you are turning on your compatriots?"

Eric laughed at the notion. "Traitor? No! I just realized that there was no value. It was not a true gambit. It would have just been a foolish move."

Davis, clearly impressed, said, "You seem well versed in chess. I find your use of it a very interesting metaphor. So, tell me, if Agent Evans and I are knights, and you and those office workers are pawns, who are the king and queen?"

"The king is insignificant. The king may be the target of the game, but he is essentially powerless. The real threat is the queen."

"And that would be me!" The fresh voice came from the doorway. All turned to regard the speaker. The woman standing there was closer to retirement age. She had pale skin, and her blonde hair had veins of silver running through it. Her face was tight. Her green eyes seemed to have the power to burrow into a person's soul. It surprised Eric that Dianne Morse, the Regional President of North America, had paid him a visit. The two agents sprang to their feet. The RP's smile was sly as she spoke again. "Well, Mister.... Larson, was it? That certainly is an interesting take on the situation."

"Madam President!" Davis was clearly not expecting the intrusion. "We were just finishing up with the interrogation."

"Have your report sent to my office, agent. I just stopped in to see how the questioning was going. But I see he is not giving much other than colorful metaphors. I doubt you'll get anything further from this man. He is obviously well trained. No, there are better uses for him."

As they walked to the door, Agent Davis turned back to him. "As the President has said, the interrogation is over. We will escort you out in due time."

Eric smiled and said to the RP, "It was a pleasure finally making your acquaintance, *Madame* President." He was sure to fill the word 'madame' with as much venom as he could. "You know, one thing about chess is that if a pawn manages to the other side of the board, it can be promoted to any other piece in the game. Even a queen. I guess it just goes to show that anybody is replaceable."

She paused as she reached the door and examined him. Her look was not too smug now, more of disgust than anything. He smiled as she exited the room. "Good luck with your speech!" When the lights turned out, leaving him in total darkness again, he just laughed. He kept laughing for quite a while after.

Chapter Four

CELEBRATION

2163.05.17 | 13:15

The railbus was packed, with many people still waiting on the platform, when Brett finally embarked. He had never seen so many people traveling at one time before. Fortunately, the UGC expected the rush and made sure that busses were plentiful and frequent enough that the lines moved quickly. After all, most people were heading to the celebration. After leaving the Columbia station near his office, the bus took thirty minutes to reach the central district of Old Washington.

History was not a major focus in the education and training of citizens under the UGC. Most of what was taught focused on the past hundred years. Prior to that, the Department of Citizen Development generalized the history of the world. Only certain jobs required a more thorough knowledge of the past, and those were limited to the higher citizens, the politicians, educators, and scientists. Average citizens did not have any need for history.

Still, Brett knew enough to know that the place he was heading to, now known as the Washington Mall, had once been known as the "National Mall" when this region was still part of the United States.

Museums that remained open but hardly saw any traffic surrounded it. As with everybody on board, he departed the railbus at the "Natural History" platform, next to the museum of the same name. It had been a long time since he was there. Most of the displays are now related to the Plague and how it evolved and affected the globe. It was also one of the few places to see animals, albeit in a taxidermic or artificial state.

Brett made his way across the platform and to the ground level. Few places in Capital Metro were at ground level, with much of the city elevated to the Rail platforms. Other than some maintenance workers and bots, the area below the rails, known as the "Undercity," was off-limits. No one wanted to go down there, anyway. It connected to the sewage and waste system and was a labyrinth of old streets. Anyone who wasn't assigned for maintenance or similar tasks was seen as suspicious if caught. Brett put the Undercity out of his mind and continued along his way.

He checked his comm device and located Lindsey on the tracker. Picking his way through the growing crowd, he soon came upon her, along with his children, waiting patiently near the entrance to the old museum. Lindsey's golden blonde hair was tied back in typical fashion for the average citizen. Though he enjoyed looking at her face, he loved the times at home when her hair would hang down past her shoulders. Olivia's hair was tied back like her mother's, but it was darker, much like Brett's own.

As Brett approached, Olivia saw him first and ran over to embrace him. She leaped into his arms, wrapped him in a big hug, and called out, "Daddy!"

Brett hugged her back, then placed her on the ground. He looked up, smiled at Lindsey, and ruffled Scott's hair, who was resting in her arms. Lindsey commented, "You were let out early. Did something happen?"

Brett looked around. Their meeting place was a little removed from the crowd, and Brett was certain that no one else was close enough to hear anything they said. Still, he remained cautious. "I'll tell you about it later. Nothing to worry about. Come on, let's find a place before all the best spots are taken."

They picked their way through the crowd. Brett had scooped up Olivia and placed her on his shoulders while Lindsey carried Scott, who had just turned two-years-old a couple of months ago. They were soon in the Washington Mall proper. There was a stage between the Washington Monument, which rose like a spire, and the grand statue of William Moore, the first President of the UGC. There were large monitors to project the ceremony across the field to those who could not get close enough. Fortunately, Brett and his family found a place relatively close to the stage, near where the camera crews were set up to record the broadcast of this momentous occasion.

The family settled into their spot on a special blanket laid out on the ground. A couple of chairs were provided for them while they waited for the ceremonies to commence. Scott sat down on the blanket, playing with a toy designed to teach basic skills. Brett and Lindsey sat in the chairs. Olivia, with a seemingly permanent smile on her face, came up to her father excitedly. "You missed the museum, Daddy! It was fascinating. You would have loved it."

"Is that so? Did you learn anything?"

"Did you know, Daddy, that people used to keep animals as pets? There was a whole exhibit that showed how they would feed and care for those pets."

"They still have that exhibit? I thought they would have gotten rid of it years ago. Could you imagine living side by side with animals? Wretched!"

Olivia just laughed. "Daddy! I think it would be interesting. I want to see an animal...a real one."

Brett shook his head. "You know animals are kept away from humans for a reason. They carry and spread disease."

Olivia looked crestfallen. It pained Brett to see her that way, but what could he do? He had to get her to clear her mind of those kinds of thoughts. With her testing only a week away, something as simple as wanting a pet could be dangerous. He looked to Lindsey for support. She smiled at him and turned to their daughter. "Sweetheart, you know your father is right. Perhaps while we wait, we should go over your skills and make sure you are prepared for next week. Now, let's begin with the basics. Spell 'mother.'"

Olivia quickly responded, "M - O - T - H - E - R."

Brett observed the quizzing with satisfaction. Olivia didn't miss a beat on any of the questions. From spelling to arithmetic to "Fundamentals of Citizenry," Olivia belted out the answers. They carried on as the surrounding space filled in. Brett looked around at the sea of people. This was the largest gathering that he'd ever seen.

Finally, at 14:00 on the mark, the ceremonies began. A horn sounded, ringing through the massive field, drawing everyone's attention to the stage. In seconds, the crowd was silent, and full attention was on the figures walking out onto the stage. Several PPU agents in dress uniform, along with security bots, emerged from the back and lined up along the edge of the stage, overlooking the crowd. Everyone stared in awe at the elegance of the uniformed officers and with dread at the menacing robots.

Three more people stepped out from the back. The tall man with dark hair slicked back and a thin mustache was Richard Sanders, Chief Councilor of the UGC-North American Region (UGC-NAR). He was the Regional President's representative in the Prime Council of the UGC in Geneva. The younger woman, Kathy Cloud, was the Chief Governor of Capital Metro. The middle-aged woman, dressed in a tight suit with a stiff cape hanging down her back, was Dianne Morse, the Regional President (RP) of the UGC-NAR. They stepped up to the podium, the first two flanking RP Morse as she adjusted the microphone. Brett picked up Olivia onto his lap, and Lindsey did the same with Scott. He took Lindsey's hand as the RP spoke.

"Welcome, citizens, to the United Global Coalition Centennial. It was one hundred years ago, on this day, that the great nations of the world, all that survived the horrible Plague that threatened our existence, came together and voted to make the UGC the sole global protector over all the citizens of Earth. They saw how well the UGC handled the crisis and knew that it was vital to maintain a global presence to ensure prosperity for all citizens. The union ended war and strife. It also helped us to build a better world for every one of you.

"As the century went on, the UGC has made great strides to further protect you, our citizens, and ensure prosperity, justice, and equality. Sadly, there are those who seek to end that prosperity. Rogue groups from the Wildlands continue to harass and threaten the stability of the world. These terrorist groups, such as the infamous Gray Roses, are abominations and no real threat to you. Every day, we are taking more of their operatives into custody, and those operatives give up the whereabouts of their comrades with ease. It is only a matter of time before these troublesome pests are eliminated for good. Then we can set about reclaiming the Wildlands, bringing about prosperity for all our citizens."

She paused as a roar moved across the crowd. Even Brett was pulled into it. He chanced a glance around and saw others in the crowd fully swept into the speech. When he glanced at Lindsey, she seemed transfixed on the RP. He looked back at the speaker as the crowd simmered down.

"Fellow citizens! Our time of prosperity is just beginning. Once, all the peoples of this Earth were embroiled in eternal conflicts with no end in sight. The nations fought amongst each other both openly and in secret while the people of the world were paying the price. Because of this folly, they did not see the threat coming that nearly erased humans from this planet.

"But we, the United Global Coalition, chose not to let that happen. We fought to protect the people of the Earth. We stopped the Plague and kept it from you. We built a system that allows all citizens to be a part of society in a productive and efficient way. We ended conflicts between nations and saw to the prosperity of all on this Earth. We will continue that fight and continue our pledge to protect the people and to expand our future.

"Citizens! Go now and celebrate! For you have earned it. Do well, and you will be well under our guidance and protection."

When she finished, the crowd erupted in a tremendous and deafening roar that surpassed the previous one. Brett joined in, caught up in the excitement. Finally, the sound died down, and the stage was empty. He didn't even see the RP or any of the others leave. He looked at Lindsey, who was looking back at him, smiling. Her eyes told a different story. He leaned to her. "What is wrong?"

"It is nothing. I am just tired. Preparing Olivia for her testing has been taxing on me, that is all."

Brett smiled at her. "Come, let us get our rations while we can." They stood up and started navigating their way through the crowd.

CHAPTER FIVE

ENCOUNTERS

2163.05.17 | 14:35

The family arrived at the ration stands set up along the outskirts of the Washington Mall. Lines were already forming, and Brett led his family to the shortest line. Within an hour, they had received their meals for the festivities and had found a decent spot to eat. Freshly grown fruit made up the bulk of the rations. The fruit was accompanied by small pieces of cake and water pouches. They divided the food and began eating.

The children were distracted by their food and some simple toys. Brett sat close to Lindsey, near the edge of the blanket that the UGC provided. He looked around and made sure that nobody else was close enough. Other families sat on their own blankets in the vicinity, but they kept a healthy distance from each other. When Brett was satisfied that no one would hear without straining, he leaned into Lindsey and spoke to her as quietly as he could. "I think we need to stop with the stories for a time."

Lindsey turned to him incredulously. "Why are you bringing this up again?"

"Olivia's testing is a week away. It is important that she stay focused."

"My father read those stories to me when I was her age. It didn't hinder my testing."

"I know!" Brett pulled back for a moment. "But she is different from you. She is smarter than you and I were at her age."

"Yes, she is smarter! She will know what to do."

"I don't think it is that simple, Lin. I am certain that they have gotten stricter with the tests since we took them. The tests were still new at that time. I am sure they have evolved."

Lindsey shook her head. "What happened to you to bring this up?"

Brett hesitated and looked around to reassure himself that nobody was close enough to hear them. "Today, one of my coworkers was taken away by the PPU. Eric Larson. Apparently, he was a member of the Gray Roses."

The news shocked Lindsey. "I remember him. There always seemed to be something off with him. He appeared friendly. But I don't know, there was something...about him. His friendliness seemed a facade." She looked back at Brett. "What does that have to do with our daughter?"

Brett's face grew concerned. "Before he was taken away, he spoke to me. He said that I should take Olivia far away from here. Take my whole family away."

Lindsey sat in thought for a moment. "Maybe he's right!"

Brett stared at his wife. "How...how could you possibly say that?"

"I don't know! I'm just worried!"

"Where would we even go? What would we do?" Lindsey did not have an answer. He continued, "It's these books that have me worried. These...fairy tales. Our daughter is smart, yes. But she is distracted. Some things that she says and does are dangerous." Brett looked up toward his daughter, but only Scott was sitting on the blanket. He jumped up and looked around. He could not see her. Lindsey was frantically searching, too.

Eventually, as a man in the crowd stepped aside, Brett noticed Olivia conversing with an unfamiliar woman. Brett rushed over while Lindsey paused long enough to scoop up Scott before following.

"My, that is wonderful! You are just a delightful little girl." The woman was stooped down, speaking to Olivia. When she saw Brett and Lindsey approach, she spoke again. "Well, Miss Olivia! It appears that your parents have come for you."

Olivia turned and smiled at them as if nothing was wrong. "Hi Mommy, hi Daddy!"

The woman stood up. She was middle-aged, perhaps in her forties. Her blue eyes were captivating. When Brett and Lindsey paused, the woman spoke up. "My apologies! I saw the young girl get up and walk away. I intercepted her so that she would not get too far."

"Thank you!" Lindsey said.

The woman waved her hand and smiled. "It is nothing. I had children once, too."

Brett looked around. "Where is your family?"

"Oh, they are far away. I am afraid I am just visiting Capital Metro for this one day. Just here for the celebration. They could not make it, unfortunately. They have their duties to perform."

"That is a shame. It was a stirring speech that the RP gave."

The woman smiled. "Yes, that was quite a speech, indeed." Her smile seemed off, though. There was something odd about her, though Brett could not place it.

Lindsey spoke up. "Can we have your name? Perhaps we could repay you for your help?"

"Oh, no need! We all must look out for each other. My name is Rachel. Perhaps we'll meet again someday. I visit the city occasionally. I work in education assessment, making sure that they meet requirements. My work frequently takes me around the region to analyze schools. And it looks like Olivia will start soon."

Brett replied, "She goes for her testing next week."

Rachel smiled. "I am sure that she will do great. There is a spark in her I have not seen in a long time. I believe she may just set the world on fire. In a figurative sense, of course. Well, I need to be going. It was wonderful to make your acquaintance." With that, Rachel disappeared into the crowd.

Brett and Lindsey both kneeled beside Olivia. Brett said sternly, "Olivia, you need to be careful and not wander off like that."

"I'm sorry, Daddy. I saw a butterfly. I just wanted to catch it and look at it."

"A butterfly? You must have been mistaken. There are no butterflies in the city. The UGC keeps the city free of all pests. Someone must have been careless with their waste. I pity them should the police bots or the PPU notice."

Lindsey cut in. "Perhaps it is time that we make our way home."

Brett looked at the sky and nodded. "That is a good idea." They returned to their area and cleaned up their rations. They gathered the blanket and dropped it off at a return receptacle near the ration stands, then left the Mall and returned to the upper platforms to catch the railbus.

When they reached the station, Brett held up a card to the robot attendant, which scanned it. "What is your destination?" the melodious robotic voice inquired.

"Housing Complex 21 H-3, Bethesda District." Brett replied.

"Proceed to platform Delta. Your bus will arrive in twenty minutes."

Brett nodded and led his family to the platform. It was not really crowded, as many people were still at the celebration. They walked to the waiting area.

As Brett looked around the platform at the other citizens, he noticed a strange man, dressed in a robe, of all things, walking in their direction. His hair, though short, was wild, as if it hadn't been combed or washed in days. It seemed like the man was oblivious to any of the surrounding people. The man froze as lights began flashing from behind Brett. Brett turned to see two police bots entering the platform and heading toward the man.

When he turned back, the man was already running the other way. The robots gave chase and quickly caught up with him. A shock rang out as one of the police bots launched a stun bolt, dropping him instantly. They restrained and picked him up, escorting him out of the platform. The bots announced, "Danger neutralized! Please return to your duties. Danger neutralized!"

Brett held his family close as the incident unfolded. With all that had happened today, he couldn't wait to get home. He stared at the track and waited for the railbus to arrive.

CHAPTER SIX

HOPE AND SORROW

2163.05.17 | 15:20

Rachel watched the family as they gathered their belongings. That girl was truly extraordinary. She could see things others could not. That was the value of innocence and imagination. It was unfortunate that the girl would soon undergo her testing. If she passed, the UGC would erase her imaginative drive through conditioning. If she did not... Well, that truly would be a waste.

The family had disappeared from her view, lost in the crowd of people. She had the girl's name, at least. Olivia Hardin. Maybe there was something that she could do. She'd have to reach out to her contacts, find out all she could about this girl and her family. What an asset the girl would make.

She felt the presence of the person who came up beside her. Or maybe it was the smell of sweet sweat ignited by the heat of the spring afternoon that alerted her. Regardless, she knew Mitch had joined her there in that corner, away from the crowd. She almost felt that they were invisible to the passersby in the vicinity. That was good, and not unexpected. The people just wanted to live their lives and stayed clear of anybody else. It was better for them.

Without turning to the newcomer, she spoke. "I take it things have not gone as you planned. I have heard no reports of any explosions."

"It seems our operative in the Columbia Data Center did not go through with his task. The Cleaners took him."

"And the others?"

"They found the Annapolis operative dead in his apartment. He never made it to the data center there. It appears that he never constructed the device and that he took his own life."

"Suicide? That will have the Cleaners curious." Suicide was essentially illegal in the UGC. Because of that, it was rare. The Annapolis operative had no family to be punished for it, so that would weigh in their favor. Still, it wouldn't take a genius to connect him with the captured operative in Columbia. Rachel shook her head. She turned to regard her companion. He was a few years younger than she was... still in his upper thirties. With his completely bald head, his goatee provided a stark contrast, lending him a sinister appearance in the shadow of the towering building behind them. His face was almost in a pout, as if he was about to throw a tantrum over his failures.

"If I were there when you set up this foolhardy plan, I would have shot it down," she said.

"But you weren't! And we had to do something today. With the celebration, we had to let them know they were not invincible. That we are stronger than they think. It would have been a symbolic victory."

"At the cost of a valuable operative. Now we are down *that* operative with no *symbolic victory* to show for it." She regained her composure. "When Joe returns, we will discuss your repercussions."

Mitch scoffed. "Joe...the great Giuseppe Valentino." The venom in his voice was thick.

"Like him or not, he is one of the founding members of the Gray Roses. And his moniker strikes fear in the UGC ranks and keeps us in the shadow."

That moniker, Giuseppe Valentino, was a name he picked himself. It was his calling card. The name was not on the approved list for the North American Region. It was too ethnic. But his true name, Joseph Lawrence, would have given him away, and it did not have quite the impact as his flashy moniker. She gave Mitch a sly eye. "And he saved your ass on more than one occasion." She smirked as Mitch cringed.

"I am one of the founding members, too, just as you are. Yet it seems like I have been relegated to *Junior Partner*." She knew it was a sore spot. He and Joe were already friends when Rachel came into their fold. When the three of them formed the Roses, Joe became the "face" and Rachel took on a shadow lead. She had connections within the UGC and was instrumental in getting their operatives in their places, whether for long-term placement or quick strikes that required surprise. Mitch hailed from the free people in the Southwest. His family had trained in tactics and war, preparing for an open rebellion against the UGC. But they were killed in an early engagement that saw the rebellion die out. Mitch survived and fled to the east, where he met Joe. She understood his feelings at being relegated to a "lesser" role.

"So, is it jealousy? We all have our part. You are valuable for your tactical mind, but it seems your emotions too often cloud your judgement of late. Today's fiasco is proof of that." She studied him. He had something else to tell her. "Your look tells me you have more bad news for me. What is it?"

"Your team returned with valuable information. However, as they were leaving the executive building, they were ambushed by some guards. The team made it out thanks to the sacrifice of your 'golden child.'"

Rachel shut her eyes and dropped her head. Oh, Kara! How was she going to break it to Jenna? "She is dead?"

"No, but as good as. They took her into custody. The Cleaners have her by now."

Rachel considered Mitch's assessment and agreed. It would be near impossible to perform a rescue mission. Jenna would want to be part of one. The two girls were practically daughters to her ever since she found them hiding in the Undercity. She took them in, raised them, and trained them. She knew the risks of sending them into the field, and so did they.

Rachel pulled her thoughts together. "Return to your post. Extract everything you can from the information. Don't let Kara's sacrifice be for naught. Joe should be back by tomorrow and we will go over our plans."

Mitch agreed and slipped away. Rachel studied the nearby crowd. It was thinning out. She had a meeting with Jenna already planned. She began her trek to the meeting place.

Soon, she arrived at the location at the far end of the Mall. It was an old monument that once held a great stature of a former American President. The Lincoln Memorial was what it was called. The statue had been removed and now the site just gave an excellent overview of the great field before it, with the old Washington Monument towering over everything in the middle. There had been talks of placing a new statue there, of some idiot UGC elite. But nothing had come to fruition yet. Rachel scanned the few people standing around the steps. She found Jenna near the top, almost hiding inside the structure.

Rachel paused as a security bot went by, making its rounds. Once it had passed, she slipped into the shadows of the structure and appeared beside Jenna. The young woman looked out over the Mall, toward the great spire monument that towered over the landscape. A pang struck Rachel's heart as she realized how much she loved her and her sister as if they were her own children. Those children were long lost, terminated by the UGC for failures to conform...because they dared to dream. It was what set her on the path that led to the Gray Roses.

Now another child was lost, and she had to break the news to her sister. Jenna did not look at her, but whispered. "This is a change. You are late."

Rachel smiled at the remark. "I had an interesting encounter. It has left me perplexed."

"It must be a real puzzle." The girl's mirth was playful, Rachel knew. Jenna turned to look at Rachel. "So, what is my next assignment?"

"The reason for this meeting has changed. I was expecting to have you take part in clean-ups to a couple of other missions, but they both failed, so we are reevaluating. As such, I do not have any other assignment for you currently. But I have some news for you."

Jenna gazed at Rachel, her eyes giving away that she already suspected the news. "It's about Kara, isn't it?"

After a moment of hesitation, Rachel nodded. "She was captured by the UGC. She sacrificed herself so that her team could successfully complete their mission."

Jenna stood there, listening. "That sounds like Kara."

Rachel admired the stoic resolve of the girl before her...and resented it, too. Still, she could see that Jenna struggled with the news, though it was very subtle. She grasped Jenna's arm and pulled her deeper into the shadows of the structure. "It is okay to shed a tear, my child. My own heart wants to burst. She was like a daughter to me...as are you."

Jenna stared at her. Wetness was forming in her eyes, but her expression remained still. "I will mourn when this is all over. When the UGC has fallen, and we have regained freedom for the world." Tears finally broke from Jenna's eyes, but her face remained stoic. "Do we know where they took her?"

"I do not have any intel on that yet. Likely the facility in Essex." She reached up and wiped the tears from Jenna's face. The girl did not retract or flinch from the touch. Rachel wanted to embrace her. But she knew that even in the shadows of the monument, that could be dangerous. She continued. "It is unlikely we will be able to launch any type of rescue."

"I didn't expect as much. And I understand. Both Kara and I knew what we were signing up for when we became operatives."

Rachel nodded her head at Jenna's words. It pained her, but she knew the girl would do her duty. "Go now, my child. Take some time. I will reach out shortly." She took a deep look at Jenna, then finally said, "Stay strong!" With that, she slipped away, leaving the girl alone in the shadows of the monument.

A couple of minutes later, she found a perch where she could again see Jenna, who was now emerging from the structure. Jenna stopped at the edge of the stairs and stared across the vast field. The crowd was rapidly dissipating as the sun approached the horizon. Finally, Jenna walked down the steps and left. Rachel watched her as she traversed the Mall.

When Jenna disappeared, Rachel turned and began walking in the opposite direction. She had a lot to do. First, she would check on the progress of the information that Kara's team retrieved. Then...Olivia Hardin. The child's name kept popping up in her mind. Yes! There had to be something that she could do. Perhaps her contact in the testing center could help? The wheels in Rachel's mind were spinning. She knew the fate of a child like that all too well.

CHAPTER SEVEN

EVENING AT HOME

2163.05.17 | 17:56

It was just before 18:00 when the railbus stopped in front of the Hardin family's housing complex. They disembarked and walked together to their flat on the third floor of the eight-story building. Given all that had happened, Brett felt exhausted. He could see it in Lindsey, too. When they arrived, they quickly settled in, putting away their remaining rations and sending the children to their room to play with the UGC-approved toys. While Lindsey took the children back, Brett sat down on the couch in the sitting room. A few minutes later, Lindsey returned and sat beside him. He put his arm around her, and she snuggled in.

"I'm sorry," Brett said, breaking the silence.

Lindsey was rubbing her hand along his chest. "Sorry for what?"

"I'm sorry for being so hard earlier. About the stories. I just…I'm worried."

"I know. I'm worried, too."

"It's just that…I sometimes wish that the moment I saw those books, I would have had them destroyed."

Lindsey stopped rubbing and looked at him. "That would have infuriated me. Those were a gift from my father before he departed for retirement."

"Gifts he had to hide to give to you." He saw the hurt in Lindsey's face. "I know! I... You know we can get in serious trouble for even possessing them."

"My father read them to me when I was Olivia's age. And ban be damned. I get such joy out of reading them to Olivia and Scott. I remember hearing my father complain about the ban. He said it was ridiculous."

"That may be, but the UGC believes them to be harmful. They corrupt children's minds. At the very least, they set children up for danger by making them think they can do things beyond their true abilities. I'm worried about Olivia's testing being less than a week away. She is smart—there is no doubt. But she is often dreamy. and you know that can be dangerous."

After a few moments, Brett continued. "Three years ago. You remember what happened? The Beacons?"

"Yes! But that child clearly had issues. He was always reserved. Some would say that he appeared to be a bit slow."

Brett stood up, then turned to stare at her. "Lin! They took him away. It was only supposed to be for a year. What happened to him?"

Lindsey looked up at Brett. She seemed so small with Brett looming over her, but her eyes were burning. "No one knows what happened. Some say the Beacons left to be with him, others say that he was terminated. But that won't happen to our daughter."

Brett snapped back, "How can you be so sure?" His tone was harsher than he meant. He took a calming breath and glanced up the hall at the room where their children played. He kneeled in front of

Lindsey and placed his hands on hers. In a much softer tone, he asked again, "How can you be sure?"

"I have been working with her. I've been telling her how important it is to keep certain things to herself. Whenever I give her a practice test, she scores very high. Only once did she slip by mentioning *unicorns.*"

"All it takes is one slip."

They sat there for a moment, Brett kneeling in front of Lindsey, holding her hands. They both looked at their hands intertwined together. Finally, Lindsey turned her face to Brett. "Why DIDN'T you destroy the books?"

Brett caressed her face. "Because I love you."

Lindsey smiled at that response. "Love." As she spoke, she seemed to grow distant, like her mind was drifting away. "We didn't even know each other when we were married."

"Are you saying that you don't love me?"

"No, I'm not saying that at all. I suppose I got lucky when we were matched." She gave him a smile. He knew what he was referring to. Some tenants in this very building were couples that just didn't seem like they fit together. He pulled her hand up and kissed it. Lindsey's face flashed to puzzlement for a moment. "I'll ask again, what stopped you from destroying those books?"

Brett sat for a minute, staring at her. "I saw your face when your father gave them to you...when you realized what was in that bin he smuggled inside. You were glowing. I just couldn't take that joy away from you."

Lindsey's smile was full of warmth. She pulled him up and wrapped him in an embrace. "I love you so much. I do."

Brett returned the hug. After a moment, he pulled back and looked deeply into Lindsey's eyes. "You're up to date on your blockers, right?"

Lindsey gave him a wry smile. "Of course! Are you?"

"What do you say that we get the kids in bed early tonight? I think we could both use a release."

Lindsey stood up; her smile was wide. "I'll start getting them ready. You get yourself cleaned up. We can put them in bed together. Then..." She let the sentence hang as she left the room. Brett smiled and stood up as well. He went to their bedroom and began preparing himself. It had been several months since they last shared physical intimacy. It would be a great way to end such a crazy day.

While Lindsey bathed the children in the main bathroom, Brett took the time to shower in their private bathroom. Once he was done, he threw on his pajamas and saw that Lindsey was getting the children into bed. He walked into their bedroom and found Olivia already tucked under her blankets, awaiting him. Scott was nestled in his crib. It would soon be time to upgrade him to a bed. He was good at staying in the crib, though. Unlike his sister when she was his age. She was climbing out before she could even walk. He looked at Olivia now, who was staring at him, waiting patiently. Her smile was wide. He loved how she looked. "Good night, beautiful!"

"Can I have a story, Daddy?" He hesitated for a moment, looking at Lindsey. Then he stood up and walked over to the bookshelf. He reached up and grabbed a book from the shelf titled *To Be a Citizen*! He took it down and began to open it up. "NO! Not that story! A *real* story!" Brett looked at her with trepidation. Finally, he turned to Lindsey and nodded. She disappeared as he replaced the book on the shelf. She returned a moment later and handed him an old book. He looked at the cover. *Little Red Riding Hood.*

Brett sat down beside his daughter. Scotty was already drifting to sleep but seemed intent on staying awake for the story as well. Brett sighed. "Very well!" He didn't want to start another argument. Besides, the sooner he could be done with this, the sooner he and his wife could spend some much-needed time together. He opened the book to the first page. "Once upon a time..." he read. Olivia smiled as he went on.

Despite his trepidations about these old stories, he was filled with joy whenever he read them to her. He adored the way her face reacted to the story. He had gotten pretty good at putting inflections into the characters as he read. She loved every word. Finally, he closed the book. Olivia was drifting to sleep, and Scott was already there. He kissed them both, then handed Lindsey the book.

She smiled as she took it from him. "Now go to the bedroom," she said as she reached up and pulled her hair down from its bun. Watching her shake her hair out got him excited. "For that, I will make tonight extra special."

Brett grinned. All his worries fled his mind. He hurried to the bedroom and prepared for a special night.

CHAPTER EIGHT

QUESTIONS

2163.05.17 | 20:38

The stale smell of the office was welcome. John Evans entered the room first, walking straight to his desk. Melissa followed at a slower pace. Her mind was on the events of the day. Apprehending Larson in the morning, dealing with the suicide in Annapolis District, Larson's interrogation, the mess at the executive building, the crazy man on at the railbus station; it all just barely scratched the surface.

The two were just returning from the transport deck. Larson and the others that they apprehended were on their way to the containment facility. Just as well. Even if they got another crack at the man, Melissa doubted they would get anything more out of him. They barely got anything from him as it was.

John stretched in his chair and rubbed his eyes. He looked at Melissa as she reached her desk and said, "I am glad to see that one go."

"You let him get under your skin. What's worse is that he knew it."

John shrugged. "You're right. There was just something about that man. He certainly didn't like me. You, on the other hand...I think he was sweet on you."

Melissa looked at him with disgust. "Please!" She sat down at her desk and logged into her terminal. She pulled up the files of those sent on the transport and studied them for a few minutes. Then she swiped a few of them away. Those were insignificant.

John leaned over to look at the screen. "More work? I thought you'd be ready to call it a day. It is already late."

Melissa stared at the remaining files. "The Roses have been very active lately."

"It's the Centennial. We expected them to do something."

"There is something more to it. I just don't know what. They clearly meant Larson and the suicide in Annapolis to be statements. They both failed to go through with it. But there was nothing at the Baltimore data center. If they really wanted to cripple us, why not hit all three?"

John scratched his chin. "As you said, they were statements, but the operatives didn't have the conviction to carry through."

"Maybe the suicide, but Larson? He has conviction, he just didn't believe in the task. He remained loyal to his comrades...wouldn't give them up."

John looked at the screen. "You think the crazy John Doe is a Rose?"

Melissa nodded. "I am certain. There are no records of him at all, except a surveillance capture at New York Metro just two days ago. How did he get into the Capital Metro?"

"And how did he get to a railbus station so close to the Mall? But we interrogated him ourselves. The man was clearly crazy. Talking about monsters near York."

Melissa nodded. "He saw something. York is referring to the community of outcasts up in the Pennsylvania Wildlands, not the Metro. Him being a member of the Roses explains how he could get in and out of metros without being flagged." She looked at the last record. "Then we have the girl."

John nodded. "She is Gray Rose, for sure."

"The question is, how did the long-presumed dead daughter of a disgraced council member go undetected for years and infiltrate the Executive building with a team of operatives? She was expertly trained, that is for certain."

"Yet she was captured."

"Captured! But her team got away with the information they acquired. Do we have any idea what it was?"

"Their data grabber hid its tracks in the system surprisingly good. At this point, it is safe to assume that they compromised all the data on the server."

Melissa acknowledged that with a contemplative nod. Unfortunately, there was a lot of information on that server that even she did not have clearance for. It would take time to sort out what would be useful to the Gray Roses... and for what purpose?

John stood up. "It's been a long day. I suggest we come back fresh in the morning. I'm going to go grab my evening to-go rations." He left Melissa there in her contemplation.

She opened a map on her terminal and pinned the events. Then she transferred the map to a larger screen on the wall, sat back and stared at it. Occasionally, she would zoom out or scroll the map to focus on different areas. Besides the incidents of the day, she looked at other incidents related to (or believed related to) the Gray Roses. The terrorist organization had been quite active in recent months. They extended all along the coast, from New York Metro down to Atlanta. Much of the activity was only discovered after the fact and only a handful of operatives were intercepted. Today had been the most successful day for the PPU, as far as apprehensions and preventions go.

Melissa studied the map. There were a lot of pins of varying colors. Red pins were the incidents like those today. Yellow pins were potential locations of Gray Rose bases. The satellite array was still a work in progress. Many satellites were antiquated or obsolete—relics of a distant past. Some were available for basic navigation and communication between regions. They didn't have any good recon satellites, so they could not confirm many of those yellow pins. Then there were the green pins. Those were known communities of outsiders, those people who have been surviving in the Wildlands since the Great Pandemic, along with those who had been exiled from the Metros.

Melissa examined the red pins in relation to the Metros and the green pins. The Wildlands around Atlanta Metro, New York Metro, and Capital Metro saw the greatest activity. Of course, those were the three most significant Metros along the East Coast of the North American Region. Incidentally, smaller Metros like Boston, Philadelphia, and Miami rarely saw any activity.

Melissa also considered the types of activities that the Gray Roses were conducting. Most of them seemed to be information gathering or recon missions. Hostile activities such as harassment and sabotage were rare. The activities had seemed to pick up as of late. She stared at the map, trying to puzzle it out.

Despite her concentration, she still heard the footsteps coming up behind her. She knew it was just John returning. She glanced over as he stepped up next to her and looked up at the map. He had his ration box in one hand and his jacket in the other hand. "Find anything yet?"

She shook her head. "You'd be the first to know if I had."

"Like I said earlier, it's been a long day. You should go home to Darren. I am sure that he is waiting for you. Don't let this eat your soul. Go home, get laid, and come back refreshed."

She looked back at him. He had a smirk on his face. "I suppose that is your plan?"

He chuckled. "Absolutely! I imagine Tina is already in bed, ready for me to walk through the door."

She patted him on the back. "Go ahead. I suppose you earned your reward."

"You don't have to tell me twice." With that, he headed out of the room.

Melissa stood there for a moment longer, looking at the map. What were the Roses planning? She had a feeling that things were only getting started. Finally, she shut off the monitor, grabbed her jacket, and headed out the door. Her partner was right. She could think more clearly in the morning.

CHAPTER NINE

CONTAINMENT

2163.05.18 | 00:12

Much like the holding cell, the interior of the transport was kept dark. Eric could hear the noises of the other passengers. Quiet sobs in one corner, heavy breathing in another. He had gotten a look at the others while they were waiting to be loaded onto the transport. There was the couple in their early twenties, apparently in possession of contraband property. Eric was certain that the man was the one who was sobbing. The kid was charged with assaulting his job training instructor. The newest addition was a man who seemed a bit loony. Eric recognized him from his time at the Gray Roses' base near Winchester before taking on his assignment at the data center. The guy was of sound mind back then. Now he was muttering something about *monsters in the woods*. Then there was the woman.

Eric noticed her as soon as she was brought into the cage where they awaited the transport. By the looks of it, she was beaten when she was apprehended. He knew little of the circumstances of her capture. There was a hint of recognition. He could tell that she had a hint of Asian blood mixed in with something else, some European culture, he supposed. His mind went to two young girls in his early days with the organization, to two mixed Asian girls that were training to be operatives for the Roses. They were Rachel's "daughters." The oldest one had golden hair. This striking woman had to be her. And she was trained well. But how could a woman under Rachel's tutelage get captured? She seemed in control of herself, despite her predicament.

The sound of the engines changed, and the transport craft swayed. Eric knew that meant that they were preparing to land. He sat there patiently as the craft came to a stop and the hatch opened, revealing lights from the landing pad that flooded the night sky. Eric cringed at the sudden sting of the lights. When his eyes adjusted, he could see beyond the platform that they were in the industrial district of Capital Metro, where all the factories that built everything from office furniture to police bots were located.

The restraining bars holding the prisoners raised them onto their feet, turned them, and automatically filed them out of the craft to the awaiting welcoming party. Two robot sentries flanked three people; an armed prison guard, a decorated female officer whom Eric identified as the warden of the facility, and some scientist-looking person. The latter wore a lab coat and smock and had medical tools.

The prisoners lined up as the warden examined each one. She silently nodded as she passed and finally waved her hand. The robot sentries moved forward to either end of the prisoners, forcing them to turn in their restraints, and began marching them into the facility. As they walked, Eric could overhear the conversation between the warden and the scientist.

The melodious voice of the warden rang out first. "These experiments of yours falling well short of your promise."

"I've tweaked the process. I can assure you of better results this time. I am sure that I have the parameters for control well in hand now."

"You had better! We are growing wary of your 'experiments.' Consider it lucky that your previous results, while far short of desired quality, have been able to be utilized for other means. Still, if you fail to produce the desired results, I will recommend terminating your endeavor."

"Need I remind you that my work here was sanctioned by the council? You have no sway!"

The conversation was lost as Eric entered the building. They were led to a room where a series of robotic arms meticulously removed their clothing. A bar moved across the ceiling and sprayed them with a substance, followed by an optical scan of their bodies. Eric knew that the substance was scan fluid that allowed the optical sensor to detect any threats that the prisoners may have had hidden. The Cleaners had already removed the detonator on him when they apprehended him, so he was not concerned.

A final spray washed the fluid off them, and a dryer ran across them to remove excess water. Finally, a man garbed in a full lab suit entered the room and looked them over one by one. Eric looked at the other prisoners as the man examined them. The newest guy seemed out of it...like he didn't even know what was going on. Eric wondered what the man saw that made him crack. The couple stared into the distance, trying to remove themselves from the situation, though the looks on their faces were of sheer terror. They understood. This was a one-way road.

The golden-haired woman stood there stoically as the lab guy scanned over her up and down. She didn't even flinch when his inspection seemed to linger over her breasts and crotch. She was clearly trained for this. The boy reacted the worst. He was squirming, obviously uncomfortable with his situation. Tears ran down his face. Finally, the man reached Eric. Eric stared defiantly into the man's suit.

It was the scientist from outside. The man responded to Eric's defiant stare with a smirk.

When he finished with his inspection of the prisoners, he turned to the nearby mirror. Eric could hear the man speak, though his voice was muffled by the suit. "They will do! All of them! Move them to the waiting cell and we will prepare the room."

The braces on their feet forced them to turn and walk to another door. The group was marched through the corridors to a holding cell. Once in the cell, the door secured behind them. The braces beeped and relaxed. The group was free to move about the cell on their own while they waited.

Benches lined the back wall, and the adjacent wall held a receptacle for their waste. The boy ran straight toward that and emptied his stomach. Eric was just glad that the receptacle flushed so that the smell of the vomit wouldn't linger in the small room. He continued to examine the prisoners. The couple huddled together, finally letting their tears silently flow. At least they were together. The other Rose was standing in the corner. Something really got crossed in that man's mind. And the boy...the boy was now cowering in the other corner, clearly weak and ashamed.

The woman, however, sat on the bench, unembarrassed by her nudity. She gave him a leer as she looked his way. Eric thought it might be worth one last pleasure in this world before he got what the UGC had in store for him. The thought was fleeting, and he dismissed it quickly. He crossed the room and sat on the bench next to her. Despite her sneer, she didn't shy away when he sat down.

After sitting in silence for a bit, the cell door opened, and two people in lab-suits entered. They looked around, then led the crazed man and the boy out, the door slamming shut behind them, cutting off the boy's screams. The couple began sobbing and embraced tighter.

Eric looked at the woman beside him and was impressed by the stoic expression on her face. The fear was nearly undetectable. It was there, but she suppressed it.

"They caught me before I could carry out my mission," he said. "How about you, *Amicus Meus*?"

The woman turned and eyed him, showing a hint of recognition. She understood the code word. Latin was a dead language, after all. They had more complex codes, but they were often departmentalized. The Latin terms were the most universal and understood among the Roses. She nodded and replied, "I stayed back while my team escaped an ambush. They took me before I could commit *Final Evasion*."

So, her team escaped while she provided cover. She was unable to take her life before capture. "I hope that your mission was successful, at least. Mine was not. Before I could make my escape, I was diverted. I could have completed it, but I didn't have the nerve...and maybe too much empathy for the saps I 'worked' with."

"Empathy? That could be dangerous."

"I was embedded too long before I got the orders. If you ask me, they were the wrong orders, anyway."

The woman put her hand on his leg. "We do what we must for the cause. Now, we accept was it coming."

Eric eyed her, then looked around the room. The couple had quieted their tears and were now on the floor, making out. They seemed to be accepting their fate and sharing their final moments together. As he sat there, he felt the golden-haired woman leaning against him. She, too, was watching the couple. It seemed her resolve was breaking a little. Many thoughts went through his head. He knew what she wanted. He put his arm around her shoulder and held her as they watched the couple making out while tears fell from their eyes. Their last embrace.

He didn't know how long they had sat there. He felt like a monster, both with his thoughts regarding the woman beside him and his voyeurism of the couple. Perhaps his resolve was breaking as well. He squeezed the woman into himself as she leaned against him, feeling her soft sobs as they sat there.

Finally, the door opened again, and the two buffoons in bio suits returned. They looked at the couple on the floor. One let out a laugh and walked toward Eric and the woman. The man spoke to his companion as he approached. "Leave the couple. The doctor wants to give them a thorough examination first. He has other plans for them. He's looking forward to these two subjects now that the two duds are out of the way."

The man stood in front of Eric and the woman now. "Stand up!" he commanded. When they didn't move, he laughed. "That is fine; we can do it the easy way." He pressed a button on a device attached to his arm. The ankle bracelets beeped, and shocks ran through Eric's body. Against his control, he stood up as every part of him turned stiff. The woman stood up next to him as well. The man laughed again. "Let's go!" he ordered, and the devices on their ankles forced their feet toward the door. Eric's arms remained free, but he couldn't move them. The shocks from the bracelet wouldn't allow it. After they exited the cell, their escorts followed and closed the door, cutting off the wails from the couple as they were left alone.

Their escorts led them through a labyrinth of corridors that took them to a steel door. When they passed through the door, Eric saw two slabs standing upright in the middle of the room. The braces forced them over to put their backs against the slabs. Puddles of something (was that urine?) lay on the floor where they stood. Metal cuffs enveloped their arms, legs, and heads, and the braces were removed. The slabs began tilting back, so that they were staring at the ceiling.

After a few minutes, Eric heard a door open, though he could not turn his head to see it. A face appeared over him, looking down with a smirk. It was the scientist from the landing pad. The man scanned them both with his eyes.

"Good morning! Yes, it is technically morning now. I am Dr. Weaver. I understand that the two of you were the hardest for the interrogators to crack. Don't worry, though! The interrogations are over. We understand that we have learned all that we will from you both."

Dr. Weaver looked beyond the pair to an unseen assistant. "Let's start with ten milligrams of nandrolone each." Eric felt a prick in the arm as they injected the needle. For a moment, his curiosity overcame his fears. What was with the steroid injections? What are they doing?

The doctor looked over them and nodded. "Yes, yes! I think it is time for the cocktail." He smiled as he stepped back, then left Eric's field of vision. A couple of seconds later, a door clicked. The assistant came into view, wearing earmuffs, and inserted a needle into Eric's arm. A long tube attached it to a drip bag above his head. Moments later, a strange sensation filled his arm where the needle was inserted. It spread quickly through his body. First, it was a tingle. Then it was like fire shooting through his veins.

Somehow, his head became free from the restraints. It didn't matter—he couldn't turn it to where he wanted. He couldn't even think of doing so. The fire inside his body was too great to focus on much else. Eventually, his head rolled over as his body reacted to the raging fire inside him. He saw the woman on the other slab. Her body was thrust forward, away from the slab, while her arms and legs remained in the restraints. Her head restraint appeared broken now. Pox marks were forming all over her body, though Eric barely gave them any thought. He noticed that her mouth was open as if in a silent scream.

That was strange. Then he realized it wasn't just her silence that was alarming, but the deafening sound of his own screams overpowering hers.

CHAPTER TEN

VOICES OF CHILDREN

2163.05.20 | 19:46

The platform was empty. It was late twilight, so that wasn't too unusual. Still, Jenna had been there for a while, and she had not seen a single person. At least, she thought she had been there for a while. She was uncertain now. Had she spaced out? That was unlike her. She had better control than that. She looked around. This platform was in the central Baltimore District. The bay was not far off. In fact, the platform was over the old harbor.

Looking down along the rail, Jenna saw the light of a railbus as it finally approached. Taking a step back from the edge, she waited for the bus to arrive. The vehicle slowed down, eventually coming to a halt right in front of her. When the doors opened, she stepped on board. There was nobody there. It was a local railbus, and it wasn't common for a conductor to be on board. Local railbuses were automatically operated. Only in the open wildlands between Metros was a person required for operation.

Typically, there would be one or two additional passengers at this hour. She walked to a group of seats near the middle of the bus and sat down, facing the front. She leaned back in the seat, and the vehicle gave a slight jolt as it started.

The darkness was thickening outside as twilight gave way to full night, and the lights from the city cast shadows throughout the interior of the railbus. The bus was heading toward the Washington District. She watched the lights go by. As the bus moved, she caught sight of a reflection in the window. She blinked. The bus was empty, but she saw a person sitting in the front group of seats on the opposite side. The lights flickered past again, and she saw the person again, a woman with her head covered by a hood, even clearer. She turned to look, but no one was there. When she turned back to the window, the reflection was gone.

Jenna glanced around. Perhaps she needed some rest after all. She rubbed her eyes and leaned back in the seat. There was a strange comfort in being alone on the bus at night. She let her eyes shut to clear her mind. Too much had happened over the last few days. Suddenly, she had a sensation that the bus was going down a slope. Jenna opened her eyes and sat up. The outside was extremely dark, and the interior lights had dimmed. A weird tingling sensation washed over her.

The bus soon leveled off. She strained her eyes to see outside, but it was too dark. What had happened? Movement brought her attention to the front of the bus. There stood a female figure with its back to her. Even in the dim light, she could see that the woman was naked. But the most striking thing was the woman's hair. "Kara?" She barely mouthed the word. She didn't even know if she said it out loud.

The figure turned toward her. It *was* her sister. Kara looked straight at her and wheezed out a single word. "Help!" Suddenly, the railbus came to a stop, jostling Jenna in her seat. When she looked up again,

Kara was gone. Jenna scrambled to the door and looked out. This was impossible. She was in the undercity.

Ahead, a single structure stood before her, an old house that she remembered well. It was the house that her mother took her and Kara to when they fled to the Undercity after their father's death. She walked toward it. It had been a long time since she had seen this place. When they built the rail platforms, they didn't even bother to demolish a lot of the structures that were below them. Unless they obstructed the platforms, most of the old structures just gained a steel sky.

When she reached the door of the old house, she looked back and discovered that the bus was not there. She was startled by that fact, but quickly put it out of her mind. The familiarity of the house in front of her muted her senses. Pushing open the door, she entered. Just like when she entered the house as a child, dust covered the floor and the remaining furniture. She could see the tracks of rats, mice, and other vermin. It was a strangely comforting thought. The first animals she ever saw were the creatures that scurried around in the undercity.

Jenna froze—she heard voices. Children's voices. She followed the sound to the room where she and her sister had slept when they lived there. There, she saw two girls lying on the floor. She let out a gasp, but the children did not seem to notice. The little one was sobbing and the older one, the one with golden hair, was crooning to her. Tears rolled down Jenna's face. She mouthed along with the words that she was so familiar with. "Love Me Tender." Kara sang it to her often to calm her down. The girl finished the song, and the younger one was calmer now. The older gently stroked the younger's back and whisper. "It will be alright. I'll always be here to protect you." The older girl looked up, her eyes meeting Jenna's. "Always! My little Jenna-bear."

***

Jenna sat up, sweat seeping from her brow, tears streaking down her face. In an effort to suppress the dream, she inhaled deeply. She was in the little apartment that Rachel provided for her and Kara. She laid back down and pulled the sheets and blankets over her. This was the bed that Kara had been using; Jenna could still smell her scent on the sheets. Despite the painful memories, it still comforted her.

She heard footsteps approaching the bed. She turned and saw a cup being held out to her. Her eyes focused on the person holding the cup: Rachel. Jenna drank deeply. Rachel reached over with a towel and wiped her brow, then sat on the bed next to her and caressed her face. "I would ask what your dream was about, but I am certain that I already know. It was her, wasn't it?"

Jenna nodded. "How long have you been here?"

"Long enough to see your distress. I know better than to disturb somebody that far into a dream. The way you twitched and shifted, it seemed intense." She gave a comforting smile.

Jenna sat up and wrapped the woman in a hug. "Oh, Rachel! When will the pain end?"

Rachel held her tight. "When you move on, it will lessen." She pulled out from the embrace and looked Jenna in the eyes. "But do yourself a favor. Never let the pain go completely. Hold on to it for the rest of your life. Let it simmer. There will be times when you need that pain. It will strengthen you in time."

Jenna took in the advice. It had been two days since the celebration...since she learned the news of her sister. She took occasional walks around the city, but mostly just stayed in her room. She thought for a moment. "You took a big risk coming here. You must have something important for me."

"I came here to check up on you. You may be one of my top operatives, but you are like a daughter to me, first and foremost. You and your sister. Your well-being is of the highest importance to me. But...you are right. I DO have something for you, if you are ready."

Jenna turned toward her. "Yes, I am."

"Are you sure?"

"Yes! I must do something. Just sitting here will not change what happened." Jenna got up from the bed and stretched her legs. "Kara knew the risks, and so did I. There will be time to mourn later. I am ready."

Rachel smiled. "That is good. The information that Kara and her team retrieved provided us with some revelations, but there were many holes. Much information has been redacted, and many referenced documents are missing."

"But that information was retrieved from the UGC Headquarters. Why would they censor the information there?"

"We have an idea where the missing files and information may be. If the information is anything like we suspect, it could really shift things and expose the truth of the United Global Coalition." There was a hint of venom in her tone.

"So, where can we find the missing data? And how can I help?"

Rachel turned to the nearby window. "We have found references to a 'black server' in a secured location. All indications are that it is in the containment facility in the Essex Industrial District."

"The prison?" Jenna thought about it for a moment. It made sense, in a way, that they would use that facility to hide the data.

"The place is more than a prison. It is a research facility and administrative building as well. But a prison makes up a big part of it."

Something else hit her. "The prison! Kara!"

Rachel was shaking her head. "I don't want you getting your hopes up. While we are certain that she was taken there, there is no indication of her status. As much as I would love to rescue her, I worry about certain factors in that facility."

Jenna sank into herself a little, but nodded her head. "What is the mission?"

"We can have you embedded by tomorrow. You will be assigned as a custodial worker. Your task will be to confirm and locate the server, gain access to it, and retrieve the information. You may have some time to dig around for our imprisoned operatives. But DO NOT compromise the primary mission. If that fails, they will likely relocate the server and we will not have access to it again."

"I understand." Jenna was pragmatic; she knew not to get her hopes up. Still, if there was a chance that she could rescue her sister... She let the thought hang. "Locating the server shouldn't be too much of a problem. Accessing it may be another story."

"Don't worry about that. Locate the server first. Once you do, I might just have the means to get you access. My...cousin works there. He is a doctor of some importance in the UGC."

"So, we already have somebody embedded there?"

"No! He is a loyalist through and through. But I have some leverage over him. We might be able to use that to our advantage." Jenna understood. "Be ready by tonight. You will be supplied with additional details along with some tools you will need to complete your task."

"How can I reach you?"

"When you locate the server, provide the information through the normal methods. I will reach out to you with the information that you need to acquire access. After that, I will go into hiding in the Undercity. Once your mission is complete, find me there." Rachel took a deep look at Jenna, then gave her a firm embrace. "Be careful.

That my cousin is working in that facility is worrying to me about your sister and our other captured operatives. Who knows what tortures they are enduring?"

"I'll be careful." With that, they broke their embrace, and Rachel left without another word. Jenna considered the mission. Aware of the unlikely odds of discovering her sister, she still held onto hope. She settled back on the bed. Although she knew she would receive little rest, she had to make an effort to get more. It was time to focus her mind.

Chapter Eleven

THE UGC AND ME

2163.05.21 | 10:50

"What year did the United Global Coalition establish the Regional Name List Act?"

Olivia barely hesitated. "2110."

Lindsey smiled. Olivia was doing excellently. She scanned through her training module tablet, looking for a tough question. "Let's see. What was the name of the first President of the UGC?"

"William Moore."

"And his successor?"

Olivia paused for a moment. "Nicole Johnson. The Grand Council elected her in 2067. One of the opposing candidates, Brian Jacobs, attempted to have her as...as..." Her face scrunched up as she tried to sound the word out. "... assassinated! The attempted assassin was terminated, and Brian Jacobs was exiled into the Wildlands. He was the first top official to have been exiled."

Lindsey smiled and clapped. "Very good. That will impress the proctors."

Olivia beamed at the praise. An alarm went off, alerting Lindsey that somebody was at the door. She checked her device and initiated a connection. "How can I help you?"

The person on the other side had on the standard uniform of a UGC official. A white bar on her shoulder indicated the lady was of the lower ranks, though still important. The lady looked at the camera and smiled. "Good day, Mrs. Hardin. My name is Jane Graves. I am here to check on the status of Ms. Olivia."

Lindsey acknowledged and tapped an icon on the device, allowing Ms. Graves entrance. She stood up and instructed Olivia to wait where she was at while she greeted the woman. When she arrived at the door, the lady was already standing inside. Her black hair was pulled back in a standard UGC fashion. Lindsey felt a bit of shame that her hair was still hanging down and free. "My apologies. I did not realize that you were coming by today."

"Oh, that is quite alright, Mrs. Hardin. This is an informal, yet important, visit. Standard protocol dictates that we keep the visit a surprise. Given that your daughter's testing is in four days, we want to check on the progress."

Lindsey was a bit rattled by the speech. "Why...certainly. Well...I was just working with Olivia." She watched the woman tapping away at her device. "Uh, that is why I am not ready for the day. I have been tirelessly working with her to make sure that she is prepared."

Ms. Graves looked up from her device and smiled. "Never you mind that, Mrs. Hardin. We like to see that you are dedicated to making sure that your child is prepared."

Lindsey relaxed a little. "Please come in. Olivia is just in the other room. I must ask that we try to keep it quiet. My son is napping right now."

"At this early hour? It isn't even noon time yet." She started tapping in her device furiously.

"He woke up very early this morning and was full of energy. I had to chase him around while his father was preparing to leave for work. With so much attention on Olivia right now, I think he's just trying to get some of his own." Lindsey chuckled.

Ms. Graves continued tapping in her device. "I see!"

Lindsey watched her for a moment. The woman's constant tapping made her uneasy. When she looked up and flashed a smile, Lindsey said, "This way." She led her into the playroom, where Olivia waited. A few toys were scattered about, but it was not too messy. Olivia was interacting with one of them, a puzzle box she had no problem opening. Lindsey gauged the woman's reaction. Ms. Graves smiled as she took a seat on the nearby bench. The smile was off, though. It looked...disconnected.

Lindsey crouched by her daughter, who looked up with a beaming smile that contrasted with the official's lifeless one. "Olivia. This is Ms. Graves. She is here to observe you and ask you a few questions."

"Hello, Ms. Graves." Olivia's face shone.

Ms. Graves gave her another disconnected smile. "It is a pleasure to meet you, Ms. Olivia. How old are you?"

"I will be five years old in four days."

"Do you know what that means?"

"Yes. I will take a test to determine what my job will be when I get older."

The woman tapped on her device for a moment. Then she looked at Olivia again. "Well, now. I have a few questions for you. We won't be long. Ms. Olivia, who was the first President of the United Global Coalition?"

Olivia looked at her mother and smiled. "William Moore."

Ms. Graves tapped on her device. "Very good. What year was the United Global Coalition established?"

Olivia paused for a moment. "It was established...on...the twelfth of August, 2042." Ms. Graves continued her infuriating tapping. She paused, however, and looked at Olivia with astonishment as Olivia continued. "It was established in response to the Great Plague to help the old nations protect against it. On May 17, 2063, the old nations voted to make the United Global Coalition the world government, effectively dissolving the nations."

Lindsey smiled as Ms. Graves stumbled over the response. "Well, that was...very good! Most children your age struggle with just re-membering the date. My! If you keep this up, Mrs. Hardin, Olivia may be placed in an excellent position in the UGC." She blinked at her own comments. From Lindsey's experience, officials never use the abbreviation in formal settings. "Oh, my! Forgive me. I shouldn't have said that. It is not our intention... What I mean is, we don't want to give any indications of greatness until after the final testing. I must apologize. Still...!"

Lindsey tried to hide her joy at the response. She didn't know whether she liked the woman's assessment or that Ms. Graves was so thrown off to make such a slip. "I understand!"

"Now, Olivia, let's move on to arithmetic. What is ten plus twelve?"

"Twenty-two."

"How about eight times five?"

Olivia only hesitated a moment. "Forty."

The woman tapped furiously on her device. "Let's see. How about thirty-two times twelve?"

Olivia sat there, thinking. The question shocked Lindsey. "I must apologize. Long multiplication was not in the Placement Test Readi-ness material."

The woman raised her hand as if to calm her just as Oliva responded, "Three hundred and eighty-four."

Ms. Graves looked down at her device. "That is...that is correct." She was clearly astonished, and so was Lindsey. "I...uh! There is no need to worry. We do not expect that the child be able to solve the problem. It is a test of its own." She seemed to space out as she finished. "The genius factor."

Suddenly, a sound from the nearby monitor indicated Scott was waking up. Lindsey checked it. "I should tend to my son. I will only be a moment."

"Yes, yes," Ms. Graves responded. "Well, we can move on to reading comprehension. Olivia, I see that you have some old-style books in your room. Can you pick out your favorite and read it to me?"

Lindsey froze as her daughter stood up and walked over to the nearby shelf. She let out a light sigh of relief, and hoped that Ms. Graves didn't notice, when Olivia returned with a book entitled *The UGC and Me*. As Olivia started reading, Lindsey excused herself to check on Scott.

As Lindsey went to the bedroom, she could hear Olivia reading fluently, which made her proud. She stepped in and found Scott holding a book. It was one of the fairy tale books. How did he get it? She grabbed it from him and picked him up before he could start crying. With the hope that the insufferable woman wasn't watching, she quickly glanced at the camera. She carefully set Scott on the changing table, collected the diapers from the shelf below, and concealed the book beneath the stack.

When she was done changing his diaper, she picked him up and carried him back to the playroom. Olivia was just finishing the book, and Ms. Graves stood up. She had clearly regained her composure.

"Well, this has certainly been a pleasure. And it is nice to meet you…"
She turned a questioning look at Lindsey.

"Scott!"

"Well, it is nice to meet you, Scott. I look forward to seeing you
in a couple of years." She tapped on her device a few more times. "I
must say, Mrs. Hardin, you are doing an excellent job with Olivia. The
United Global Coalition shall hold high hopes for this young lady."

Lindsey believed the woman was being genuine. "Thank you." She
set Scott down on the floor and gave him a toy. "Let me see you to the
door." She led Ms. Graves to the entrance. The woman was tapping
furiously on her device as they walked. "Thank you for coming by,"
Lindsey said, opening the door.

"Yes. I must say, it was an enlightening visit. We look forward to
seeing Olivia's results on the test."

Lindsey closed the door behind her and looked through the eyehole
to ensure that the woman was leaving. She watched as the lady walked
down the stairs, tapping on her device. "It's a wonder she doesn't fall
and break her neck," Linsey said quietly to herself. She turned and
walked back to the room with the children. Scott was busy fiddling
with a shape toy. "Olivia, come with me for a moment."

Olivia stood up and walked to her mother. She seemed a little timid.
"Did I do something wrong?"

Lindsey took a glance at the room before responding. "I have a few
questions for you." She led her to the sitting room. They both took a
seat on the couch, and Lindsey turned to her daughter. "Sweetie, did
Ms. Graves do anything while you were reading to her? Did she look
at the monitor?"

"No, Mommy. She just sat there while I read the book."

"Are you certain?"

"Yes, Mommy."

"It's okay, sweetheart. I have another question for you. Do you know how Scott had one of your special books in his crib?"

Olivia shrank into herself and muttered. "I was reading it to him while you were in the shower this morning."

Lindsey patted Olivia's shoulder. "Okay, sweetie. But you must know that you need to be careful with those books. We could have gotten into a lot of trouble if Ms. Graves had seen it."

Olivia looked ashamed. "I'm sorry, Mommy. But why would we get in trouble?"

"Because some people don't like those books. They think they are bad."

"Why would they think that?"

Lindsey stared at her daughter. "Because they had bad parents."

Oliva pondered for a moment. She looked up at her mother. "I am sure glad that I don't have bad parents."

Lindsey let out a laugh. She reached over and hugged her daughter. "No. You have wonderful parents. Your father and I love you very much." She stood up. "You can go back and play. You did a wonderful job today. I am proud of you. Your father will be, too, when he hears."

Olivia stood up as well. "Okay, Mommy." She rushed over and gave Lindsey a quick hug, then ran back to the room.

Lindsey watched as she ran off. When Olivia disappeared into the room, she walked back to the bedroom and dug out the book from where she had stashed it. She looked at the cover. *Jack the Giant Slayer and Other Tales.* She thought about that story about a boy who climbed a beanstalk and took on a giant. Sometimes, she wished she could be Jack, who outsmarted the giant and defeated him.

She remembered her father reading that book to her when she was a child. Back then, the ban on these books was still relatively new, and her father had never liked it. He hid the books away. She didn't know how he managed to smuggle them to her house. He was planning for retirement and Olivia was still a baby.

She wished there was a way to talk to him. Since he was moved to Miami, she hadn't heard a word from him. She knew that wasn't his fault. The UGC felt it best that retirement be solitary. She hoped he was still alive. Likely, the UGC would notify her of his and her mother's passing. But there hadn't even been a word from them.

Lindsey looked at the book in her hand. Today was too close a call. When Brett got home, she would have him take them down to the incinerator in the building and destroy them. She considered the stories in the book. "Jack the Giant Slayer," "Cinderella," "Goldilocks"... She realized she didn't need the books. She had read them so many times as a child, and even now, reading them to Olivia and Scott over the years, that she could practically recite them. They would live on. And once the testing was done, she could tell her children the stories and all would be well.

But for now, she had to focus on Olivia's test.

Chapter Twelve

The Maze

2163.05.21 | 22:18

"You'll get used to the layout soon enough." The man walked slightly ahead of Jenna through the corridors of the containment facility. "It's a little confusing at first, but you get the hang of it quickly."

Jenna was already building a mental map of the place. From the entrance lobby to the administrative offices and the various offices and spaces in between. She studied every detail as she passed. It was one thing that she was good at. She knew it was likely why Rachel wanted her on this mission, despite what it could mean. Her sister was here somewhere. But Jenna couldn't do anything about it. She couldn't compromise the primary mission. She would do her duty.

The man, Spencer Curtis, stopped in front of a set of double doors at the end of a short, wide corridor. They were in an offshoot of the main cross corridor. There was a single door on the side wall of the short corridor, with a red light (currently off) above it. The double doors at the end appeared thick. "Your badge will get you into almost anywhere in this facility except past these double doors."

"What is past there?"

"The holding cells of the *prisoners*." The way he said the last word was strange. She detected a bit of disgust in his voice. "The only people that go back there are the guards. Them and the robot sentries."

Jenna noted she had not seen too many robot sentries along the way. One was in the lobby, a couple more were patrolling the hallway. "I'm surprised there aren't more of them...the robots, I mean."

Spencer stared at Jenna. "Most of 'em are behind those doors. Keeping the *prisoners* in line." Jenna could hear the disgust in his voice again, and it was thick. "Don't worry! Once prisoners are processed, they are kept in their cells." He pointed to the single door with the light. "That is the door that you will be concerned with, but we will get back to that. I'll show you the intake first. Come on."

As they walked down the corridor, Jenna asked, "What are in the rooms on this side of those doors?"

Spencer scratched his sandy beard. "Mostly offices and labs. This facility doubles as a prison and a research center. What a better place to conduct high-level research and experiments than an already secured prison? The UGC is efficient in that way." Leading her, he walked down the corridor and then turned into another. He scanned his badge, and a door opened to the outside. He stood at the doorway and pointed out. "That is the landing pad. Transports come in and unload the prisoners. They are taken through another door into the facility." He closed the door without going through and walked to another one along the wall nearby. He swiped his badge again and entered, waving her to follow.

Jenna followed him into a dimly lit room. There were a couple of guards at a station in front of a window. The window looked into another, brighter room that contained a series of robotic arms. "This is Intake-A. Prisoners are stripped and scanned for bugs and other...things. You know, weapons and the like."

Jenna stared at the intake room with all the robotic arms and beams. She imagined her sister standing in there, being stripped by those arms. The thought disgusted her. "So, I will have to clean that room?"

"No, not that room. The robots take care of it, along with the lazy guards in here."

"Nice to see you, too, Spence." The guard chuckled.

"What, Mikey?" Spencer replied. "Everybody knows you are the laziest guard here." The other guard chuckled and went about his work. He pressed a button and one beam activated. Steam poured out of the holes in the beam, filling it almost instantly.

Mikey spoke up. "We just processed a few intakes. You had best get your little friend here to the lab and show her what she will do there. The doctor is waiting to process this new batch. You know that buffoon doesn't like to wait."

Jenna saw the hint of disgust in Spencer's face again. It was subtle, but it was still there. He guided Jenna through one door into a side hallway, then rounded the corner into another small hallway. Jenna continued trying to build her mental map. "This place is definitely a labyrinth."

Spencer stopped. "A what?"

"A maze."

"Like I said, you'll get used to it. They designed it that way in case any prisoner somehow got past the double doors. They would need extreme luck to find their way out. Of course, that was before—" He cut off. He turned down another corridor and stopped in front of another guard, who was sitting on a bench across from a door. "Good evening, Frank."

The guard looked up from his snooze. "Spence! Is this the new night custodian? A pretty thing, too." The guard had a slightly thin mustache and a beard that went straight down from the middle of his lips and exploded once it reached his chin. Jenna thought it was rather stylish for a guard. It was something she'd more likely encounter among the free peoples.

"Yep. She's filling in while Sharon recovers from her illness."

"Right, right! Well, for all I care, Sharon should immediately retire when she recovers. I wouldn't mind seeing this face every night."

"You know you shouldn't flirt with the new help. Especially since your wife is right there with you. You could be brought up as having wanderlust and find yourself on one of Dr. Weaver's slabs."

The guard looked surprised at the statement. Then he held up his hand and looked at it. Suddenly, he let out a laugh before settling back on the bench and returning to his snooze. Jenna could hear him chuckling under his breath. Spencer waved Jenna over to the monitor. He tapped on the screen a few times and brought up a view inside. "If it didn't have *guests* inside, I'd take you in. You never go in when it is occupied." He pointed to a light above the door that shone red. "Anyway, you'll have to come in here once it's cleared to clean up. There is often a lot of fluids people leave as they await their fate."

Jenna looked at the monitor and saw that there were a couple of different angles displayed. There were eight individuals in the room, and all of them were naked. She didn't recognize any of them. She knew it was unlikely that her sister would be among them. Kara would have been processed days ago. The people meandering around the room were of varying ages. Five males and three females. A couple of them, both a male and female, could be no more than their late teens.

Frank the guard looked up. "A healthy bunch today. The doctor will be pleased by the specimens he has to work with." Jenna noticed a wince on Spencer's face. Whatever it was that the doctor was doing, Spencer didn't seem to like it. "This is the first group since the last batch a few days ago. He's excited to get started."

Spencer jumped at the mention of the doctor. "We best get to the lab." He led her further down the corridor. He made two lefts and a right before coming back to the main corridor. When they arrived at the double doors, he pointed further down the cross corridor to a solitary door. "That is the observation room. Dr. Weaver is often in there. He has an office inside that you will also be responsible for cleaning."

"Observation of what?"

Spencer's face froze. "Follow me." He led her to the single door next to the double doors. He scanned his badge and led her inside.

The room was nearly empty except for the two slabs in the center of the room. There was also a reinforced steel cabinet near the corner. Jenna swallowed a lump in her throat. "What do they do in here?"

"This is where Dr. Weaver performs his experiments."

"Experiments?"

"A special cocktail that he uses on prisoners. Sanctioned by the higher ups in the UGC, of course." He looked like he was going to say more, but held himself. Perhaps that large mirror that filled up most of the nearby wall made him hold his tongue. "In any case, this room requires a lot of cleaning after the prisoners are processed here. It's not uncommon to find it filled with piss, vomit, and shit. Any maybe a little blood. You'll want to wear bio gear in here to clean." Jenna was surprised to hear such vulgarities. She was used to them in the company of Gray Roses, and in the Wildland communities. But citizens of the UGC never uttered those words.

A voice came over the speaker. "If you are done with your little tour, I would like to get on with my work!"

Spencer responded, "Yes, Doctor Weaver." He waved Jenna along and they left the room in a hurry. He led her past the door to the observation room and turned left down another passage. They walked along in silence. Spencer stopped at a black door and pointed to it. "That is the only door on this side that you will NOT have access to."

"What's behind there?"

"I don't know, and I don't care to know. You need the highest of clearance to enter."

Jenna was shocked. It couldn't be this easy, could it? Well, locating the room was one thing. Now she needed to gain access. If it was that secure, it had to be the room she wanted. Spencer led her further down the hallway. At the end was a small door with no badge reader.

It was a small room and contained a cart with cleaning supplies. "This is your 'office.'" he said. Jenna looked around. There was not a lot of room. Shelves lined the one wall that contained additional cleaning supplies. The other side had hooks for clothing, one hook already occupied with a set of bio gear, and an open locker for personal belongings.

"My office? Does anybody else share this space?"

"Not really. Sometimes daytime custodians may come in here for supplies. You'll be responsible for restocking at the start and end of your shift."

Jenna studied Spencer. His face was drawn, as if he were contemplating something horrible. "What of Doctor Weaver's experiments? I noticed you don't seem to like them?"

Spencer gave a half-smirk as he responded. "You'll learn soon enough. When the prisoners are given the cocktail, it changes them. They lose their soul. It is a horrible sight. It's even worse to face them. They are filled with a primal rage. They are strong and ferocious and can rip a person to pieces in an instant. I've seen it happen."

The news twisted her gut. "That is the fate of those prisoners waiting in that holding cell, isn't it?"

"We've come to calling them *terrorlings*. The newest batch from a few days ago…there is something different about them. Unlike the first ones, they seem to have some smarts. There is a fire in their eyes."

"What happened to the first ones?" Jenna figured that she already knew the answer. She had heard the rumors coming in from the Wildlands. She heard about the carnage at that manor that left no one alive, including Jordan, a friend from her training years.

Spencer confirmed it. "There were about fifty of them. They were all released in the Wildlands around Capital Metro. A few in the north, some in the west, and some in the east." He turned to the door. "You'll be responsible for cleaning the offices in this section of the facility. That shouldn't take up too much of your time nightly. You will also clean the lavatories and the areas that I showed you, as needed. I'll leave you to get settled."

After Spencer left, she sat down on the small bench. She had no doubt about the fate of her sister now. She took a deep breath and let it out. From what Spencer had said, her sister was close by, but was no longer herself. It filled her heart with sorrow and rage. She straightened up and took another breath. She had work to do. Jenna hoped that whatever was behind that black door was what they needed to bring the UGC down. The UGC would pay for what they had done.

CHAPTER THIRTEEN

BLOOD ON THE FLOOR

2163.05.22 | 00:48

The last of the prisoners was finally subdued and being taken to their cell. Dr. Alex Weaver looked through the window into the room where a guard lay bleeding out. The brute strength of the creature that caused the guard's wound amazed him. Dr. Weaver turned to the woman beside him.

Michelle Jansen, the warden of the facility, did not look happy. "That is another guard who will be out of commission for weeks, if not months."

"Perhaps they should send some better trained people here instead of the half-wit louts we keep getting lumped with." Alex was tired of the woman's constant dismissal of his work. It was important work, and she kept trying to obstruct him.

Michelle scowled at him. "We have wasted resources on your precious project for years. And now, we are losing valuable personnel. It doesn't matter how 'half-witted' or 'lazy' they are. We are already down half of our security bots. Their electronics were irreparable and had to be sent to the factories for scrap. I am *tired* of your ridiculous notions."

"Yes, yes, I know all that. Do I care? You keep forgetting that my work has the blessings of the Regional President. And we are making significant progress."

"Progress? You are nowhere near the super soldiers that you had promised."

He glared at her. "No! Not like I had promised. But they are super soldiers in their own right. Excellent for the front line. With the space program nearing readiness, they will make excellent shock troops to wipe out the pathetic Wildland population so that we can start reclaiming it. The recent test release of the first group has been successful."

Michelle turned back to the window as the medical team removed the guard from the room. Doctor Weaver noticed that the guard's body was covered. He mentally shrugged it off as Michelle spoke. "Your creations are monsters. There is no way of controlling them. And these latest ones..."

"Monsters, but they have their uses. Do you think President Morse will weep over one guard when these *terrorlings* are so effective?"

"As I said before, the cost has been far greater than one guard. Not to mention that the prisoners can be rehabilitated and sent back into productive use instead of turning them into base monsters. I am filing my recommendation to terminate this insane project."

Dr. Weaver laughed. "You do just that, Warden. Word it exactly that way, too. Let's see how far your recommendation gets."

The warden stormed out of the room, leaving Dr. Weaver stewing in his thoughts. She struck his every nerve. He long stopped thinking of her as pretty, his disgust with her having grown so thick. She had never been a fan of his work. Sure, there were some mistakes, but that is the nature of science. Trial and error. Her feeble mind could not comprehend the possibilities. Even failures can yield unexpected success.

He looked through the window at the room. Blood and human excrement covered the floor where the guard had fallen. He pressed a green button on the console in front of the window, then turned to a terminal where he logged in and began updating his notes on the events.

A few minutes later, Spencer Curtis came in with the new custodian that he was showing around earlier. Weaver inspected the girl. She couldn't be over twenty-two or twenty-three, he supposed. Studying her, he noticed a hint of mixed ethnicity. That kind of thing was irrelevant to the UGC. But it was noticeable, especially in the North American Region.

There appeared to be a bit of Asian blood in her, perhaps Japanese or Korean. He found it intriguing and eerily similar to a subject he had on his slab recently. It had to be a coincidence. Her uniform was tight to her body. Dr. Weaver did like that about UGC apparel. It seemed to hug the women, revealing their curves. She was a little light in the chest, but that didn't matter. Her buttocks appeared ample enough.

He realized the pair were just standing there, waiting. "So, this is the new custodian?"

"Yes," Spencer answered. "She is here temporarily to fill in overnight."

Dr. Weaver nodded. "Very good. The procedure room needs a good cleaning. This evening's procedures were particularly messy." He noted a flash of a grimace on Spencer's face. It was gone so quickly that he barely caught it. "Is there something wrong, Mr. Curtis?"

"No. It will be a good indoctrination for Miss Simmons here." He turned and started instructing the girl. Dr. Weaver went back to his work as they left the room.

He put the girl out of his mind as he entered the data and reviewed his logs. There was something about these latest subjects that caught his attention. He first used the latest cocktail on the group that was brought in a few days ago. The first subjects were a young, timid boy and a crazed man. After minutes of agonized screaming, he had noticed that they had kept some of their previous traits. The boy stayed on the slab, timid as can be, despite his enhanced state. The crazed one ripped out of the restraints, his own arm coming off in the process. When the guards moved in to subdue him, he lashed out with his remaining arm and instantly killed one guard. Three more pelted him with tranquilizers, but this only enraged him more. He attacked the boy, tearing him to shreds. Never before had Weaver witnessed one of the creatures attacking another. It took an hour to clean up that mess and attach new restraints to the slabs. They went through so many restraints here.

The next two were different. After their dosage of cocktail, when they finally stopped screaming, they just sat there and stared at the mirror. They never ripped the restraints. It felt like both were staring right at him. Perhaps they could see through the mirror with their advanced vision. He entertained the thought that they might be successful and in control. But he could see a burning in their eyes, as if they hated him. But they were easily subdued to move to their cells below.

The final two, a married couple, were the most interesting of all. After the administering of the cocktail, they remained timid like the boy. When they were released, they ran around the room and settled in a corner together. Whenever anybody approached them, they were fiercely defensive. It was like they knew they were together before and were protecting each other.

Yes, there was a hint of intelligence in them. Was it some memory of their former lives? Or just an echo of sentience? The doctor could not say. This latest group produced similar results. Only the last one created any significant carnage. The woman had underlying mental issues. But they put none of the creatures down and only one guard died.

Yes! While the cocktail did not produce the results that he was seeking, it produced something more.

The door to the procedure room opened, and the custodian entered with her cart of tools. She had the added protection of the bio gown. It was a bit of a disappointment, but he expected it. Those gowns were not as nice to look at. Dr. Weaver watched her as she went about her work. She went first to the slabs to clean up the excrement. Using a fat hose, she sucked up any solid matter and scrubbed the floor with a long-handled brush. After she finished, she looked up at the mirror for a moment. There was anguish on her face.

After the brief pause, she turned her attention to the blood where the guard had fallen. Using a thinner hose with a rubber squeegee, she sucked up the excess blood into a different container on the cart. Her back was toward him, and the gown opened just enough to reveal her back as she bent down to clean the blood. She wore her uniform underneath, of course, but he stared greedily at her buttocks. Images of her on one of his slabs filled his mind. The thought made him tingle.

When he snapped out of his daydream, he realized she had finished and already left the room. He looked around. Fortunately, nobody else was there to see him as he gawked at the girl. He regained his composure and returned to his work. Satisfied with the data, he logged off the terminal. Then the door to the observatory opened, and the custodian walked in. She had removed her bio suit and stood there in her regular uniform. Only she now had the standard UGC jacket that hid the curves of her chest.

The girl said, "I am finished in the procedure room. Is there anything else you would like of me?

It took the doctor much self-restraint to stifle a grin. Oh, the possibilities that popped into his brain. "No, dearie. That is all for the night." He couldn't tell if she grimaced or smirked. Was she reading his mind? Impossible. She nodded and left the room.

He turned to the door that led to his office. There were still tasks awaiting him. He had to write his report to the Office of the Regional President. He wasn't going to let that half-brained warden undermine the effort he had put into his work. No. He had to make sure that this program was not only secured but also expanded. Perhaps the collar device could be of use. Yes, he would perfect that and that would solve the problem. The neural shocks would establish the needed control. Then the UGC would have foot soldiers with the original cocktail and field generals with the second cocktail. All he had to do was get a working prototype. That would be easier than altering the formula of the cocktail.

First things first. Get that report written and submitted. This was going to raise his standing far above that bitch warden. Dr. Weaver smiled as he went into his office.

Chapter Fourteen

EXTRA RATIONS

2163.05.24 | 15:20

Rain drizzled down as Brett exited the railbus. It wasn't a heavy rain—more of a mist. It didn't bother Brett. He was a little late getting home from work. The ration box that he carried was the reason. It was rare to get an extra ration box. As he was leaving work, Mrs. Houston gave him the special chit to use at the ration depot for Olivia.

He walked up to his apartment in the housing complex. He was excited for Olivia, but he was nervous. In less than twenty-four hours, they would know the results of Olivia's test. How would she place? When Lindsey told him about the events of the other day, he was so proud. He was very surprised when Lindsey told him to take the books to the incinerator. That was a big step.

When Brett opened his apartment door, all seemed quiet at first. He stepped in and walked past the sitting room to the dining room. By then, he was hearing voices coming from the playroom, Lindsey's and Olivia's. He smiled, set the box on the small table there, and followed the sound of the voices. In the playroom, he found Scott on the floor, struggling to get a cylindrical block into a container with several holes.

His frustration grew as he made multiple attempts to fit it into the triangular opening.

Olivia and Lindsey were sitting to the side, facing each other. Lindsey was firing off questions ranging from math to vocabulary to UGC society. Olivia answered each without hesitation. Lindsey even threw in a few math problems, and Olivia only paused a moment before giving an answer. He smiled, watching the pair.

A yell pulled his attention back to Scott. The boy had his hands in the air in triumph. It looked like he was able to fit the cylinder into the proper opening. "Way to go, Scott!" said Brett, and rushed over to give him a congratulatory hug. Olivia was clapping for her brother's achievement, and Lindsey was smiling widely.

"How long have you been here? Why didn't you say anything?"

Brett smiled. "Not long! I didn't want to interrupt you. You were doing a great job, Olivia. It seems I have good reason to be proud of both of my children today." He ruffled Scott's hair and squeezed him in another hug.

Lindsey walked over to Brett. He rose to his feet and embraced her warmly. "You are doing such a wonderful job."

"You seem really happy." Lindsey squeezed him back, then pulled away to look at him.

"I am! I have a wonderful family." Lindsey could do nothing but smile in response. "I have something for you, Olivia."

"What is it?" the child asked.

"Come and see." Lindsey picked up Scott as he led his family to the dining room. He opened the box and produced a cake. It was not very big, but enough for the four of them to share. Olivia's eyes widened when she saw it. Even Scott started kicking in anticipation. "Happy birthday, sweetheart."

"But my birthday is not until tomorrow!"

Lindsey responded, "Tomorrow is going to be a big day, so we will celebrate tonight with the cake. Happy birthday!"

They sat at the table and ate the cake. When they finished, Lindsey said to Olivia, "Take your brother into the playroom and show him some toys. I want to talk with your father."

"Yes, Mommy." She went over to Brett and gave him a hug. "I love you, Daddy." She led Scott away from the table.

When they were out of sight, Brett spoke up. "Are you as nervous as I am?"

Lindsey chuckled. "You can't even imagine."

He took hold of her hand. "You have been working hard. I meant what I said. I am proud of you."

"You don't know how much it means to me to hear you say that." She stood up and sat on Brett's lap, wrapping her arms around him.

Brett held her tight for a moment. He couldn't explain it, but it was as if he could feel love radiating from Lindsey at this moment. He didn't know how much time went by before she sat back. She stared into his eyes, smiling. "How has she been doing?" he asked.

"You saw. She has been doing excellently with the questions. She's going to place well, I know it. And we will be moved from this apartment to some place better. We could be raising a future Regional President. Who knows...maybe even a Grand President?"

Brett laughed. "Let's not get ahead of ourselves."

Lindsey shared the laugh and hugged him again. "As far as the *other* thing...not a mention. Not all week! She's been great. I was worried when we had the books destroyed. But she has accepted it without complaint. I just—"

Brett put a finger to Lindsey's lips, cutting her off, and smiled. "I love you!"

She froze. After a moment, she smiled back, then said in a hushed voice, "I love you, too." She leaned forward, wrapping her hand around the back of his neck, and pulled him in for a deep, passionate kiss.

He had thought a long time about his assigned wife. He remembered how awkward it was when they were first matched eight years ago. Brett didn't know too much about how the matching process worked. He supposed that there were some factors that went into it—age, location, status, etc. In large part, it was a lottery. The matching season took place in March of every year and started when people were in their late teens. Not everybody was matched right away. Some, especially because of their job assignment, were not matched to well into adulthood, if at all.

It took Brett until his third year to be matched with Lindsey. They had never met. He remembered how nervous he was when they had their first date. He was struck by her simple beauty right away. She had her hair pulled back in a simple ponytail, and her green eyes sparkled with life. Faded freckles dotted her cheeks; her lips were a soft pink and glistened in the light. Brett was awestruck by her face alone. And there was an edge about her that intrigued him.

Lindsey, on the hand, was indifferent to him. She later confided in him she was not too excited by him. He was too plain looking. He kept his dark hair to the ideal UGC standard. Besides his looks, he was a conformist. It was a slight area of contention. Her family griped about UGC rules and regulations. Brett followed the rules to the letter. At least, that was how she took him from the start. Perhaps it was true. Perhaps his desire to please her and be a good husband allowed him to give way a little.

During their mandatory one-year engagement, they gradually grew together. He found his time with her thrilling. It awakened a part of him he'd never known, and she enjoyed that. They grew to like each other, and that soon turned to love. At the eleventh month point of their engagement, the UGC officially issued their final approval of the union.

Brett felt the moisture from Lindsey's lips as she pressed them against his. Her tongue teased him as she pulled closer to him. A giggle from the side broke the moment, and they broke off the kiss. Olivia stood in the door frame, her hand over her mouth as she stifled her laugh. Brett looked at Lindsey. Her cheeks were now a deep red. She cracked a smile and looked at Brett as she stood up from his lap; the smile turning a bit flirtatious. "Is there something you wanted, young lady?" she said in a mock pretentious voice.

Olivia giggled again. "I thought you got lost. I came to find you."

"Well!" began Lindsey. "I'm right here. And you have five seconds to hide before I come get you. One..." Olivia let out a gleeful scream and ran toward her room. Lindsey finished counting, then chased after.

Brett followed to find Lindsey tickling Olivia on the bench in the playroom. Scott laughed with delight. "And what are you laughing at?" Brett said, as he fell upon the boy. Scott wiggled and screamed with laughter as Brett's fingers found his tickle spots. After a few minutes, the tables turned, and the children were tickling—or attempting to, in Scott's case—the parents.

The joy carried on through the evening. When they tired of the tickle fight, they settled down and ate some rations, then played with some toys together. Brett and Lindsey put the children to bed and went into the sitting room, collapsing on the couch. Lindsey nestled into Brett's arms, and he held her tight.

After a few minutes, he turned to her. "You have five seconds to hide before I come and find you."

The smile she flashed back was fully flirtatious. "Oh, you will know exactly where to find me, sir."

She stood up as he said, "One!" then ran off down the hall. When he reached the count of five, he chased her to the bedroom. He reached her as she was in the middle of pulling off her clothes. He did the same. They finally tumbled into bed and began making out, their hands caressing each other with passion and love.

By the time Brett fell asleep that night, he was the happiest he could remember being in a long time.

Chapter Fifteen

THE FACILITY

2163.05.24 | 23:15

He had a steady flow of subjects over the last few days. There was now a total of twenty-six of the "enhanced terrorlings" in the holding cells, along with six normal prisoners that Dr. Weaver deemed unfit to be processed. The last few days had been productive indeed.

Then there was the strange note. It was written on paper (of all things), folded in an envelope with his name on it, and left in the pocket of his jacket. How could it have gotten there? He discovered it that morning as he was preparing to head to his apartment. He tried to think of everybody he had contact with the night before.

His preoccupation with work was so intense that he couldn't remember anyone who came near him, except for the warden. He doubted that *she* would have left the message. He couldn't think of who it could have been.

Dr. Weaver paced back and forth in the lavatory. He slipped his hand into his pocket and produced the message. He had read it several times, and now he thought there was no doubt who the originator was.

My Dearest Alex,

It has been too long since we last spoke. It saddens me that we parted on such bad terms. You and I have things left unresolved between us. Do you remember the times we spent together? How I'd help you with your puzzles? I know how much you loved it when I leaned over your shoulder to look at your tablet. You were so protective of me. You followed me into the washroom and stood guard. I could always count on you! I do so hope that you can forgive me. One does not choose their associates. Just know that you will always have the key to my heart.

Loves

Dr. Weaver looked at the nearby mirror. His mind went back to his youth, to the days he spent with his cousin. Rachel had moved in with his family in their penthouse flat. Her parents had died in a terrible railbus accident. He was twelve years old, and she was a couple of years older. And she was beautiful. Every time she smiled at him filled him with such warmth. How he adored her.

Before she came to live with his family, he had never thought about women. Science was his only love. But she did something to him. She awakened his lust. She caught him spying on her once. He had gone on the roof of their living quarters to work on his drone. He was exploring the area between the buildings when the signal got lost and the drone fell onto a fire escape. As he went to retrieve it, he spotted her through the window. He could not take his eyes away. She was completely naked before a mirror, brushing her long hair out. He had experienced feelings he had never felt before.

When he finally noticed that Rachel was looking back at him, he freaked out. He sprinted back up to the roof. He felt extremely embarrassed. Making a dash for his room, he hopped onto the bed and quickly hid under the sheets. He was so ashamed. Tears rolled down his face. When he heard the door open, he froze. Soft footsteps approached, and he felt somebody sit on the bed next to him. He dared to pull the sheets off to find Rachel sitting there smiling at him. "You forgot this, Alex!" she had said, handing him his drone. She was wearing a robe that fell open as she leaned forward.

Yes, she had awakened him.

Dr. Weaver looked at the note in his hand. There was a wet spot on the note now. He reached up and wiped his eyes dry. He never cried anymore. It was a few years later, when he went to the science academy, that he learned she had died. She had married and birthed children. However, due to complications with their development, the UGC made the difficult decision to terminate them. It was said that Rachel was so stricken with grief that she threw herself from a platform into the Undercity. He hardly believed it. And now...this note was proof that she was still alive. And she was a member of the Gray Roses. That had to be the case. He considered the situation. His lust was bad enough. He was not high enough in the UGC for his vices to be overlooked. Not important enough. He was working to elevate himself with his experiments. But having a connection to the Gray Roses on top of that would be the last spark to light his pyre.

He reached into another pocket and produced an access card. He had decrypted the note. "Key to my heart" and "washroom" were keywords that led him to where he presently stood. He did not know the purpose. But he knew Rachel had the edge on him. The only way that she could still be alive is if she was with the Roses. It was troubling. Between that and his childhood lust for her, he was in a dangerous position. As he began to gain momentum, she had the power to plant information that could bring him crashing down.

The access card held his attention as he stared at it. He obtained a one that couldn't be linked back to him. The card was high-level clearance. It gave access to all the rooms in the facility, save the prison. It did not concern him too much. The fact that the Gray Roses would soon be doomed would nullify any information acquired through its use. He placed the access card in the sink and left the lavatory.

Dr. Weaver navigated the corridors of the facility back to the observation room. When he entered, he was surprised to see Spencer Curtis. "I thought you had left hours ago." The man spun as the doctor entered, as if startled. "What are you doing?"

"I...I was just going over the work of the new custodian, Simmons."

Dr. Weaver nodded. The girl was adequate at her job. She cleaned well. How building maintenance conducted their business was of no concern of his, as long as they did not impede his own work. Spencer excused himself and left the room. He was an odd fellow. As soon as he left, Dr. Weaver tried to put him out of his mind. He had to refocus himself. He unlocked his office door and walked in. Grabbing the schematics from his desk, he walked over to the workbench. The prototype for the control device was coming along. In a few days, he could start testing it. His fortune would certainly change then.

***

The cart's squeaky wheel echoed through the long corridor. Fortunately, there wasn't anybody nearby to complain about the noise. It was well after midnight. Another round of prisoners was brought in earlier, and Jenna had to clean the procedure room. There wasn't a lot of blood, but the other *matter* was abundant. She would have rather cleaned the blood and gore.

The number of prisoners being brought in alarmed her. Were there really that many "lawbreakers" in Capital Metro? To her knowledge, none of the more recent prisoners had been Roses. Since her first day, the guard, Frank, let her look at the prisoners in the holding cells before they were processed. She didn't recognize any of them. As far as she knew, they were ordinary citizens. Which meant that the city was full of lawbreakers or...

Or the UGC was looking for any excuse to bring in people for these transformations.

That thought did not sit well with Jenna, but neither did it surprise her. She pushed the noisy cart along the corridor. She had just seen the doctor hurrying back to the observation room. As soon as she saw him, she went to grab her cart. Hopefully, he left the item in a good place. Jenna still didn't know if he could be trusted to deliver.

Just as she was passing a side corridor, a form emerged from it and collided with her cart, almost causing it to topple. She prevented it from falling over and spilling its contents with her quick reflexes. "Julie Simmons!" said a startled voice.

Holding back a wince from the use of her alias, Jenna glared at Spencer. "What are you doing here? I thought you left hours ago?"

"I...I just...needed to stay late." He gathered himself together and looked around. "Where are you heading? Aren't you supposed to be cleaning the offices?

"I have to clean a spill in the lavatory."

Spencer blinked at the response. "Very well! Carry on." He walked off without another word. Jenna watched him leave. Something seemed wrong. Why was he here? Since she started, except for her first night when he was showing her around, he always left precisely at 2200, not a minute later.

She turned back to her cart and made sure it was straight. Whatever was going on with Spencer was a distraction. She had work to do. With luck, she could finish her mission and be done with this forsaken place tonight.

She turned down the small corridor toward the lavatory. She opened the door and pushed the cart in. When the door closed behind her, she blocked it with the cart and immediately began searching. A quick glance confirmed he did not leave it anywhere out in the open. She went to the nearby urinals and began looking in each one. The urinals were curved at the bottom and intended for either sex. After she had done her sweep, she checked the sinks. When she reached the third sink, she found what she was looking for.

Jenna picked up the access card. She couldn't believe he actually left it. She hadn't seen Rachel since the night she received the assignment. A messenger gave her the note to slip into the doctor's lab coat pocket he had left on his chair the previous evening while he prepped the prisoners about to be processed. She slipped into his office to plant the note. When she left the office, a lab assistant was sitting at the console. Fortunately, he was so intent on watching the administration of the doctor's cocktail that she was able to get out again.

She tried not to look at the victims as she did. What she saw, even briefly, horrified her. The prisoners were strapped to the slabs and had just received the cocktail. They were thrashing, their heads pulled free from the restraints, their faces locked in agonizing screams. Pox appeared on their skin, which was itself taking on a grayish hue. Jenna didn't want to look. She rushed out of the room, not caring if the door banged as she went.

Jenna snapped back to the present. She clutched the access card, then stowed it in a pouch on her uniform. Unlocking the brake on her cart, she moved it out of the way, opened the door, and pushed the noisy thing back into the corridor.

Jenna didn't want to seem in too much of a hurry, but she maintained a rapid pace down the corridors. She hoped that nobody else came running out. The noise of the squeaky wheel should warn them. It briefly occurred to her it should have warned Spencer earlier, too. She shook him out of her mind. She knew he would be another obstacle to completing this mission, but she would deal with things as they came.

Finally, she reached the custodial room. Pushing the cart inside, she looked down the hallway before entering. There was a security bot making its rounds, right on schedule. Closing the door, she got to work immediately. She stripped away the terribly itchy UGC clothing and walked over to the locker. Grabbing a black outfit, she stepped into the aramid fabric pants and pulled the shirt on. The clothing hugged her body. She fastened a belt with several pouches down around her hips, then pulled on a thin vest, also made of aramid fibers, but slightly thicker than the clothing. There was a special liner inside the vest that would be of great use.

She twisted a couple of times, testing her maneuverability. When she was satisfied, she placed the keycard in one of her pouches and checked the contents of the others. The device she needed was there, along with a couple of weapons. Pulling a hood on the shirt up over her head, she pressed a button on the vest. It activated the liner inside, which emitted a signal to scramble her appearance on cameras and make it difficult for the security bots to get a lock on her. The vest was a rarity, a wonderful gift from Rachel when she went down south.

She pushed open the door and investigated the corridor. It was clear. She left the small room and began running down the hall to her target: the black door.

Chapter Sixteen

THE BLACK DOOR

2163.05.25 | 00:18

The corridors were ominously still as Jenna reached the black door. She knew that the security bot would make its rounds soon, so there was no time to waste. She held the access card up to the scanner, and the light turned green as s the locking mechanism clicked. Jenna slipped into the room and quietly shut the door behind her.

The room was medium-sized—larger than the custodial closet, but smaller than the observation room. Several rows of racks filled the room, each rack filled with computers, battery systems, and other components. The sound of fans filled the room, creating a constant hum, while Jenna could see her own breath in the chilly air.

She scanned the racks and found a terminal. Reaching into one of her belt pouches, she produced a data stick. She plugged it directly into a port on the terminal. The terminal's screen beeped as boxes flashed up, then went away. Finally, the terminal indicated her successful login, and a prompt appeared, requesting the target to be copied.

She moved the prompt aside and looked through the system. She tapped the screen, glancing at documents, images, and videos, and explored various folders that the files were kept in. Some files and documents gave her hope. She was certain that this server was an archive that dated back to the early days of the UGC. She came upon a folder entitled "XRST," one of the scientific names referring to the Great Plague. Everything inside that folder was encrypted.

Jenna smiled. She returned to the copy prompt and selected everything. Within moments, a progress bar popped up, slowly filling as the data copied to the device.

All of a sudden, a loud bang startled her from behind. The screen on the terminal flickered and all the fans in the room quieted. As the server batteries kicked in, the room resounded with a chorus of beeps. Jenna looked at the screen. The terminal was still on, and the copy routine was still running. Its current progress was at 18 percent.

Thoughts raced through Jenna's mind. What caused the power outage? She didn't believe it was because of her accessing the terminal, since it was still active. The progress bar slowly filled as time ticked by. 20 percent...25...30. Even with all her training, she was sweating. She dared to go over to the door and place her ear to it. Overall, she was aware that there were approximately thirty individuals present at the facility, excluding the prisoners. She was aware of one security robot stationed in the lobby and another one patrolling the administrative halls, but she was uncertain about the number of active ones behind the double doors. As she listened at the door, she heard feet running, followed by shouts, though she could not make out the words.

She returned to the terminal and checked the status. 53 percent. Several loud pops rang out in rapid succession. It sounded like gunfire. Jenna went to one of her pouches and produced a gun. She checked it over. The energy pistol was effective enough if she had to shoot her way out. Her isolation in the server room had her on edge. Though she appeared safe now, not knowing what was going on outside of the room was nagging at her. The power should have been restored.

The bar was getting close. It was at 81 percent now. The sweat on her brow was thicker. 84...87...90. A gut-wrenching scream echoed from the corridors. The sound made her stiffen as she felt the goose bumps rise on her arms. Terror swept across her face. It couldn't be.

96...97...98. Jenna could feel her heart pounding in her chest...almost hear it. 100 percent. The copying was complete, and the device ran a final routine. She considered yanking it out but did not want to damage it as it loaded a virus into the terminal. A present to leave behind. It did not take too long, fortunately, and the box vanished, indicating that the routine was completed. She pulled the device from the terminal and replaced it in her pouch.

At the door, she listened. There was no sound. She cautiously opened the door and peeked out. The corridor was empty and dark. The main lights were off, with only emergency lighting showing the way. She slipped out and closed the door behind her, looking both ways down the corridor. She took a moment to examine her mental map of the facility to get her bearings. Then she began running toward the main lobby.

As she turned into a side corridor, she saw a figure enter further ahead. It slowed as it saw her. It was Frank, the guard. His terrified face crinkled in confusion for a moment. She noticed he did not have a weapon. As she considered ways to maneuver around him, a shape suddenly struck him from behind. When he hit the floor, she could hear the distinct snap of his spine. The shape leaped on top of him.

Jenna backed away. The creature was lacking any garments, and it happened to be male. The dim light revealed its grayish skin. It grabbed Frank's head and began repeatedly bashing it on the floor, cracking open his skull. Jenna was running back the other way before it had finished.

Her mental map of the facility was lost to her now. She ran through the corridors and turned down random intersections. Finally, she made it to the main cross corridor that led to the landing pad. She slowed when she neared the double doors.

A sound ahead turned her stomach. As she approached, she heard bare feet slapping on the hard floor. A shape emerged in front of her from the corridor that led to the doors. From its profile, she could see that it was another male. It turned away from her and began walking toward the landing pad. Jenna eased over to the nearest door, the observation room. She tried the handle, and the door opened. The terrorling had stopped. Not daring to breathe, she melted into the doorframe and watched as the creature slowly turned. Without hesitation, Jenna pulled herself fully into the room and quietly closed the door behind her.

Chapter Seventeen

Horrors Unleashed

2163.05.25 | 00:45

Spencer smiled as he walked past the open cells. He thought he was a dead man several times. As it turned out, the hardest part was making it to the power room. The badge that he had swiped from Mikey worked well. The idiot guard didn't even realize it was gone. When he discovered it was missing, he chalked it up to being misplaced in the barracks. He had gone to look for it when Spencer left him.

Once he was past the doors, he knew his path was set. There was no turning back. The sole guard at the door was sleeping. Nobody ever came through the double doors unless scheduled. After that, though, was where it had gotten trickier. Robot sentries traversed up and down the cell block corridors. He had to time it right to get to the other side.

The whole way, he could hear the guttural noises from the terror-lings. They seemed excited, like they could sense something was up. That helped, because both security bots and human guards focused most of their attention on the creatures. When he made it to the power room, he went to work quickly. He flipped a switch here and pressed a button there. The power levels were intensifying. From a pack on his back, he produced a metal rod.

He thought about what led him to this moment. He had worked at the facility for a long time. When they brought in Dr. Weaver and initialized his special project, he was mostly indifferent. He thought it was a waste of resources to experiment with the prisoners when they could be rehabilitated and returned to society as productive followers. But who was he to question? He did his job and nothing more.

The event that set his path took place a year ago.

He had fallen in love. In the world of the UGC, it was a forbidden love. He was not matched with her. He wasn't matched with anybody, nor was she. Crystal was his subordinate, but that made it easier. She had loved him back; he knew. They would slip away into secluded sections of the facility and make love.

He remembered running his hands through her black, silky hair as he kissed her deeply. The soft feel of her ivory skin as he caressed her while she kissed his bare chest and worked her way down was exhilarating. Even the innocent moments filled his heart with joy, like the times when they would retreat to the custodial closet and she would sit on his lap and fall asleep, her warm breath tickling the hairs on his chin. It pained him to keep their relations a secret, but that time was the greatest of his life.

Then came that fated event. He was in the observation room while she was in the procedure room cleaning the mess from Dr. Weaver's latest subjects. The wretched man was in there while she was cleaning. Spencer was cleaning in the observation room when he looked up to see the doctor got close and whisper something to her. As he did, he placed his hand on her lower back and slowly slid it down. Her anger led her to slap him in the face. She was fiery, and that fire spelled her doom. She went running from the room, but the guards caught her a few minutes later.

Later that week, she was on one of the doctor's slabs. The doctor told Spencer that he knew of his secret relations with his subordinate and had him in the room to watch. Spencer was horrified as he watched the woman he loved turn into one of those monsters.

The roar of the static building in the power room brought him back to the moment. He tossed the rod into the battery array. Sparks started flying instantly. He bolted out of the room. There was one last thing to do. The guards and bots had spotted him and were closing in as he ran. He could hear the sparks snapping and cracking from the power room. Some guards grew wary, but the bots did not slow. He reached out and pulled a switch on the wall. A moment later, something struck him to the ground. That was the first time that he thought he was dead.

He realized it wasn't the bolt from the security bot that hit him; it was the blast from the power room. The fire from the power room and the sparks of the downed security bots illuminated the room. Several of the closest guards lay dead. Spencer pushed himself up and saw that his ultimate goal had been accomplished. All the cell doors were open.

The living guards pulled themselves from the ground. He knew they were scanning for him. One got a bead on him and raised his weapon. This was the second time that he knew he was dead. But the blast never came. One of the terrorlings slammed into the guard and began ripping him apart. That was when chaos erupted.

Guards were running as the terrorlings chased them down. Spencer smiled. He knew Crystal, his lost love, wasn't among this group. She had been taken weeks ago to the Wildlands. Spencer shrugged it off. He was seeking revenge in her name. He started walking along the cells.

He froze when a shape stepped in front of him. The male terrorling looked at him, its gray skin casting an eerie reflection of the flames. As it stared at him, this was the third time that he knew he was dead. Then it seemed to smile. The creature turned away and ran off. It joined the other terrorlings as they rushed to the double doors.

Spencer walked along. The creature knew he was their savior, that he was the one that freed them. Not for the first time, he wondered if the things had any bit of their past knowledge...their past lives. He kept walking. He arrived at the cells of the only prisoners that were still human. Those that were not deemed worthy of the process. They were either too crazy or too timid.

He looked at them and laughed. One stayed in its cell but was hooting and hollering, a female whose mind had snapped. She appeared to be relishing in the chaos. The others, male and female alike, young and old, all huddled in their cells, crying. "Do not be afraid!" he assured them. "You are free now. Go!" He did not wait to see if they listened. He just kept walking, slowly making his way back to the double doors.

***

The dim glow of the emergency lights made the observation room creepier than it already was. As Jenna looked through the window to the procedure room, that feeling was enhanced by the lights that highlighted the two slabs in the center of the room, swirls of dust glimmering above them. A noise pulled Jenna's attention to the door at the back of the room. She stepped into the corner of the room and stood, gripping her weapon.

A figure emerged from the room and rushed over to the console. She eased her grip on her gun, but kept it at the ready. Dr. Weaver didn't seem to notice her. He carried a tablet in his hand and was fumbling with a wire, connecting the device to the console.

Jenna quietly approached behind him and peered at the tablet. On the screen was a layout of the facility. She knew then that it was an emergency override device. The doctor intended to use it to access the facility's systems during the power outage and change the status of doors. If the power wasn't restored before the batteries ran out on the servers, it would lock the doors and other controls into place. He pulled up the cameras and scanned each monitor. Blood and gore plastered some of the halls, and others were empty. One camera view showed the remains of what Jenna assumed was the security bot. Other cameras showed the terrorlings stalking through the corridors.

Jenna crept up as close as she dared to the doctor. "That could come in handy." The reaction of the doctor would have been comical in other circumstances. He jumped back, dropping the tablet on the console, and spun in her direction, then fell to the ground, trying to regain himself. Fear plastered his face as he inched back away from her along the floor. Jenna reached out and grabbed the tablet. A quick scan confirmed it was not broken.

Dr. Weaver stuttered, "Y...you! You're the custodian. Julie Simmons!" His face. "You are the one responsible for this? Do you know what you have done?"

"Me? I've done nothing. I am just trying to find my way out of here alive," she said.

The doctor considered for a moment. Then he said, "We can escape together. I have safe houses we can go to."

She flashed him a smile. "You would like that, wouldn't you? Rescuing the poor custodian girl. Maybe she would show you some gratitude. Let you do things..." Her face twisted to disgust as she pointed her gun at him. "I don't think so!" He flinched back. "I know that you've been watching me these past few days. Rachel told me a little about you. Your eye for her in your youth."

"Rachel? You know Rachel? She IS still alive! That means... she... you...Gray Roses!"

"I don't know what you are talking about."

The doctor's face lit up. "You can get me to her. I have nothing now. But I can be of help to you."

"You would forsake the UGC?"

He looked around. "I already have. My work is over. That bitch warden will be happy."

Jenna thought for a moment. Perhaps... "No! That would not be possible."

The doctor's face sank in despair. "Please! You must help me. I'll do any..."

Jenna fired her gun and the energy bolt swept just past the doctor's head, cutting him off. Fear plastered his face now. "No!" Disgust dripped from her voice. "You made a fatal mistake that warrants no help from me. I have no doubts that my sister is now one of your creatures."

"Sister?"

For a moment, Jenna conjured up an image of Kara in her head. "My sister...her vibrant golden hair flowing like sunbeams around her face."

"Golden hair? I..." The doctor shrunk down. He clearly recognized the description.

Jenna shook her head. "No, I will not help you escape. But for your cooperation, at least, I will leave you with a gift." She secured the device by strapping it to her arm, then disconnected a pouch from her belt and placed it on the console. "This is a tool that I hoped to never have to use. It is for when all hope is gone. I think you need it more than I do." The doctor eyed the pouch but did not move. Jenna walked to the door. She glanced at the wretched man. He appeared frozen with fear and despair. She opened the door cautiously and peaked out. There was no sign of the monster.

With a last glance at the doctor, she left the room.

The corridors were eerily quiet. She navigated her way down the main one. As it wound around the guards' barracks room, she peaked around the corner to see a couple terrorlings meandering around by the door to the landing pad. Dismay swept over her. She went back along the main corridor and then took a side corridor that she knew would lead her to the lobby.

As she approached an intersection, a naked man charged out from a side corridor and stopped three meters in front of her. Jenna froze. She did not know if she could get her gun up in time. For a moment, he just stood there studying her. There was a hint of familiarity in the man, as if she had seen him before. But the gray skin and twisted face from the doctor's cocktail made it difficult to place him. The creature tilted his head at her. Then, just as suddenly as he appeared, he ran on through the cross corridor.

Jenna did not wait to contemplate why he'd behaved like that. She took her good fortune and bolted down the corridor until she reached the lobby.

Pieces of the lobby robot had been scattered across the floor. Blood and remains of a couple of guards were splattered near the main doors, which remained firmly closed. It looked as if they'd been trying to pry the doors apart by hand. She sought a terminal behind the nearby desk.

She connected the device to the terminal's interface. In moments, the tablet connection turned green, and she navigated to the main entrance. The door was marked red on the map. She tapped it with her finger, and a prompt came up asking for confirmation. She agreed, and the door icon turned green as a loud click echoed through the room. The door opened wide. Jenna rose from behind the desk and found a figure standing before her.

The figure stood there, watching her. It was naked and clearly female. The light fell on it in such a way that she could clearly see the details of the creature. The hands had sharp, claw-like nails and gray skin. Jenna felt like she'd been struck in the gut. The creature's hair, though caked with blood and grime, had a golden reflection in the lights of the lobby. But the eyes erased any uncertainty from Jenna's mind. Despite her every instinct, Jenna slowly approached the creature.

It continued to study her as she moved, their eyes locked together. Jenna pushed her fear to the back of her mind as wonderment took over. She knew those eyes well.

"What have they done to you?" she whispered. The creature continued to stare. "Do you recognize me? Do you still know your baby sister?" The creature's head tilted as it stared; a soft growl, almost like a purr, emanated from its throat. "Do you remember holding me on dark nights? Protecting me? Do you remember the songs you sang to me to help me sleep?" Her voice remained calm even as tears welled up in her eyes. "I swear to you, dear sister. I swear they will pay for what they have done."

She continued her approach and began reaching out an arm toward her lost sister. She jumped back as the creature lurched forward with a hissing roar. When it finished, it turned and ran to the entrance. Jenna stood there, terrified and furious. The creature that was once Kara stopped at the door and gave a shrieking scream into the facility, then turned and fled the building. Within moments, a few more creatures came running through the lobby, exiting the building. Then a string of them rushed by. Some looked at Jenna—one even roared as it passed. They darted into the night. Jenna was too awestruck and terrified to count, but she estimated that well over twenty creatures ran past.

To her shock, the final shape to emerge from the corridor was all too familiar from the past few days. "Spencer!" Jenna called as he jogged past. But he just kept going without slowing or even turning to acknowledge her.

Jenna was dumbfounded. She walked over to the door and watched as the creatures scattered into the night. She did not see where Spencer had run. In the shadows, she saw two beads of light, the glowing reflection from the eyes of one monster, looking her way. After a moment, the creature turned and ran on along the railway. "Oh, Kara! They will pay! Until then, wreak hell on them all."

Lights started flooding the platform outside of the facility. Jenna looked up to see several craft closing in on the building. The Cleaners. She ran to the side, seeking a stairway leading down. They were located throughout the Metro at key locations, and she knew there had to be one here. Sure enough, she found it as she rounded the corner of the building. It was across from the landing pad for the prisoner transports. The stairwell housing had a gate blocking access. Fiddling with her belt pouches, she pulled out a key scanner and held it to the access panel for the stairway. The access opened with a click. When she looked back, she saw two of the craft releasing several rectangular objects onto the platform behind her. The objects stopped just before hitting the platform and unfolded into police bots. Before they could lock onto her, Jenna rushed down the stairs into the Undercity.

Chapter Eighteen

THE UNDERCITY

2163.05.25 | 01:30

The platforms and railways loomed overhead, giving the Undercity a sky of concrete and steel. Beams of light pierced through the gaps above, like glowing pillars standing in the otherwise stifling darkness. Jenna reached the ground and ran to put distance between herself and the access stairs. As she did, she pulled a cloth strap from one of her belt pouches that quickly fastened it around her head, covering her eyes. After pressing a soft button on the side of the strap, her vision filled with a brilliant light that only lasted a second. The sensors of the dark-vision strap allowed her to see through the darkness. As her eyes focused, she could see the base of the buildings that stretched above the platforms, as well as long-abandoned buildings that did not reach the platforms.

This was the Undercity. Jenna was very familiar with it. As a child, she hid here with her sister, scared of the world above. After Rachel found them, she took them in and raised them, but she also trained them on how to survive. The Roses had safe houses throughout the Undercity. They could hide for weeks down there without being found.

She looked at the structures surrounding her. Some were the bases of buildings from the upper city. There were also great stanchions that held up the platforms and railways. Others were old houses and businesses that had been built over. The ground was comprised of patches of dirt and pavement. Ration cartons littered the ground in some areas. Littering in the upper city meant a hefty fine that could even lead to prison time, but that did not stop many from just casting their trash through the gaps to the Undercity.

Jenna often tried to imagine what the area looked like before the upper city was constructed. She tried to picture the fields of grass that covered the dirt. She was glad that the Wildlands still had grass and trees and animals. The Undercity had some animals, mostly pests such as rats. Where people once walked and conducted business and lived was now just a sewer.

Jenna came to a stop and looked back. She saw four relatively large objects falling from the upper city near where she entered. The police bots unfolded and began scanning the surrounding area. She darted behind an old storefront.

The containment facility was at the eastern edge of the city. The city wall was just beyond the industrial section. She searched for buildings that provided access to the upper city. They would have doors where the maintenance workers and bots would access the Undercity. She walked around cautiously until she found the nearest building foundation. She jogged to the building, keeping a wary eye out for the police bots. When she reached the entrance, she quickly located the access point: a wide door that lifted. It was manual and not locked, but opening it caused a lot of noise. She lifted it slowly, trying to keep the noise to a minimum, then crawled under the door and looked around.

Jenna smiled. She had found what she was looking for—a mainte-nance vehicle. She climbed into the open-topped contraption and activated it. It was a relief for her to see that it was fully charged and ready to use. Pulling up the navigation display, Jenna took the controls. Her foot found the acceleration pedal. When she was confident, she left the car and shoved the door open all the way. The racket it caused certainly would have alerted the bots. She jumped back into the vehicle and hit the acceleration. Right when the vehicle burst out of the access port, a police bot emerged from the corner.

The bot crashed into a nearby building after she clipped it. She was fortunate that the bots had split up on their search and that the vehicle was made of tougher material than the robots. She used the navigation display to get her bearings on the Undercity roads. When she reached the main road that cut through the center of the city, she glanced back and noticed that the other bots were alerted and coming toward her. Two were still far back, but a third was quickly gaining on her.

She cruised down the road past a group of refugee shacks from the Great Plague. She checked her mirrors; the robots were a good distance behind but seemed to be catching up. Checking her navigation, she was relieved to see that she was nearing the main road.

As she pulled onto the old, large road, marked with a faded sign reading *95*, she maxed out the vehicle's speed. She could feel the tremble of the car as the needle approached ninety. In the sparse light, she saw the buildings were becoming more numerous. Behind her, the police bots were closing the gap. One was close enough for her to make out its full form in the limited light. She would have to get off this road soon. She knew that the tunnel that it led to was no longer usable.

The lights of the vehicle illuminated a green sign that read *150 Eastern Ave* and had an arrow pointing to the upper right. She pulled the vehicle over to follow that sign. As the vehicle went along the ramp, another sign came into view that read *West Highlandtown.*

The transition onto the city streets of Old Baltimore required her to reduce speed. This allowed the bots to make great gains as they followed her. One was close; its metallic voice demanded that she stop. Jenna reached into one of her pouches and pulled out a low-grade EMP. She activated it and tossed it behind her. She could hear the small "pop" as the EMP triggered. The closest bot was caught fully in the EMP field and crashed immediately. She checked the mirror; the remaining two bots had to slow down to maneuver around the blast. She picked up speed as she passed a brick sign reading *Greektown*.

Much of the old city was left intact as they built the platforms above. Only buildings taller than the platforms were knocked down if they couldn't be incorporated into the new city. At one point, an open field of dirt spread out to the right. Jenna knew it had once been an old park. The trees and grass were gone, sunlight eternally blocked by the platforms above. With the remaining bots once again getting closer, she turned to cut across the old city park.

Clouds of dust and dirt filled the air behind her, engulfing the police bots and obstructing her view. This maneuver would barely hinder them, but she hoped it would buy her a little time. She had some familiarity with this part of the Undercity. Her navigation system was giving off alarms and trying to direct her back to the roads. Finally, she made it to the north side of the old park and got her vehicle back onto the paved road headed west. Almost immediately, a police bot emerged from the dirt cloud behind, gaining speed as it adjusted to the pavement.

She pressed forward, the bot right behind her. Old buildings lined the street as she sped by. The police bot was right behind her and keeping pace. "Stop your vehicle!" it ordered. She kept going, passing many small intersections with minor roads. She could tell that she was in the downtown area of the old city. Most of the buildings here went up past the platforms and were incorporated into the new city.

The bot reached out and grabbed the rear of the vehicle. Jenna checked the navigation. Another side street was coming up fast. She cut the turn sharply, the tires of the vehicle squealing as she did. The sharp turn took her dangerously close to one building, but she was able to straighten out the vehicle before slamming sidelong into the old structure. She heard a crack behind her and glanced behind to see the arm of the bot still attached to the vehicle, but the bot was nowhere in sight. The maneuver worked. Another quick turn to the right got her heading west again.

There was no sign of the last bot as she drove down the new street. Lombard was the name, according to the navigation. Jenna drove along slowly now. She could see the old harbor between buildings on her left. The platform stretched out over it. She turned another corner, heading toward the harbor. As she approached the last street before the water, the last police bot came out in front of her and turned in her direction. Its lights flashed.

Jenna floored the accelerator and steered right at the bot. Just before impact, she leaped from the vehicle, rolling across the pavement before finally coming to a stop. Both the vehicle and the bot went careening into the harbor, sparks flaring when they hit the water.

Jenna did not move. Her body ached from the roll. Her clothes protected her to an extent, but she knew she would have some bruises. She mustered the strength to raise her arm. Gradually, she regained control of her body and rose to her feet. Although she wanted to keep the vehicle for a little while, she would have had to get rid of it soon anyway. Walking over to the waterfront, she saw the vehicle and bot sinking beneath the murky water.

Satisfied, Jenna turned and started walking. There had to be another vehicle somewhere nearby that she could use before more bots showed up to investigate. Whatever the case, she wanted to put as much distance between her and the scene as possible. With luck, she should be in Laurel District by the morning.

Chapter Nineteen

THE CLEANERS

2163.05:25 | 02:27

Agents in white protective suits scrambled about the facility. It had been an hour since the team of PPU agents and officers arrived. Bodies of fallen guards were bagged and lined up in the lobby. As Melissa walked the corridors, she noted the splatters of blood that covered the walls and floors where the guards fell. The agents were now going through and cleaning up the gore. They had already catalogued and marked the locations. This was the most horrific thing that Melissa had ever seen since she became an officer in the PPU.

The various offices and research rooms that made up the bulk of this part of the facility had all been swept and secured. Much of the team was in the prison cells below. They reported that the battery cells were destroyed, and an engineering team was brought in to connect a generator to the backup relay. That would restore power for a time, but it would take a long time before this facility was operating again.

Melissa took a breath and quickly shoved a cloth to her face. Despite the cleanup in progress, the rancid smell still permeated through the facility corridors. She looked at the tablet in her hand. Reports were still coming in. There were a couple of custodians unaccounted for, one of which was not even supposed to be at the facility during the incident.

"Agent Davis!" She looked up at the source and saw the silhouette of her partner, John Evans, coming toward her. "It is taking some time to get the power restored, but the engineers were able to hook up temporary generators to some key systems. Cameras and servers are back online. We have agents going through both."

"Have they found anything yet? What of the whereabouts of the missing staff?"

"It appears the T-1 server room was accessed shortly before the power outage. But the camera only detected an anomaly in the corridors at the time that the door opened. The Maintenance Facilitator, Spencer Curtis, accessed the prison cells shortly before the power outage. Because of the blast from the battery cells, the cameras in that area are taking longer to restore. Regardless, he is the prime suspect for the power outage."

"What of his motivation? Is he a member of the Gray Roses?"

"We are still determining that. The sole survivor told us that Mr. Curtis has been at the facility for longer than a decade. He also mentioned an affair with one of his subordinates, who was caught stealing rations."

Melissa pondered the information. It painted a solid picture of Mr. Curtis being responsible, but there were still a lot of questions. "I think I should speak to the doctor myself. Any word on Michelle?"

"She is in route. She should arrive shortly." With that, John turned to lead her to where the lone survivor of the massacre was found. Melissa was surprised that Michelle was away during the incident. And a bit thankful, too. She liked Michelle...a sound person and an excellent choice to run the facility. She had learned that the Warden had a meeting with the RP herself.

Evans opened the door to the observation room and led the way in. She took in the room with a quick sweep. A console lined up next to a large window that looked into an operating room of some type. There was a door in the far of the room. The survivor, Dr. Alexander Weaver, sat in a chair near the console, a PPU officer standing nearby, guarding him. The doctor was rocking as he sat. Melissa had seen him a couple times when she made a tour of the facility but had no interactions with him. She turned to John. "What has he said so far?"

"Nothing really. He told us about Mr. Curtis, but beyond that he was tight-lipped. He claims it is beyond my clearance."

Melissa nodded. "Dr. Weaver! Can you tell me what happened tonight?"

The doctor looked up at her and laughed. "You? No. I cannot. My work is classified at the highest level."

Melissa was only slightly annoyed. "Doctor. I am from the Protection and Preservation Unit and the lead investigator here. I can assure you that my authority is from the office of the Regional President." She held up her badge. "Consider this as my clearance."

The doctor scowled at it. "The power went out!"

John stepped forward. "You can start answering questions or the Warden will tell us about it, in which case you will be transported to the facility in New York Metro just like this. Only you won't be working there. You will be their special guest."

The doctor looked up. "The Warden?"

"She is on her way now."

Dr. Weaver shook his head and laughed pitifully. "She would be happy about that."

Melissa was growing wary of his pompous attitude. She opened her tablet and pulled up the doctor's information. Most of the data was marked "Access Denied." Whenever she put in her credentials for override, it reiterated the denial.

John's comm device went off and he answered it. After pulling up his own device and studying it for a moment, he transferred it over to Melissa's. "The engineers recovered footage from after the outage. You should see this."

She opened the footage. A hulking beast of a man, naked, stalked through the corridor. His skin was a pale gray and his hands seemed to end in sharp claws. Another clip showed a guard running down the corridor. As the guard passed an intersection, a creature similar to the first lunged out and started tearing the man to shreds. The guard's body armor provided little protection.

"What is this?" she asked, showing a still of the first creature to the doctor.

He cringed. "That is...a prisoner. He escaped during the power outage. All of them did."

She thought back to when she first arrived. "Doctor, I was told of a couple prisoners that were caught on the railbus platform ran out of the facility. One of them was taken, but he wouldn't speak. The other leaped from the platform into the Undercity. They found her mangled from the fall, barely alive. Three prisoners escaped through the landing pad exit. They have not been recovered yet. One more prisoner was still in his cell. She was found laughing maniacally." The doctor squirmed. She continued. "That is six. I was informed that the facility had a census of thirty-two prisoners. Where are the rest? What happened to them?"

The doctor twitched as he looked around the room. "That... On the monitor... That was one of them."

"What exactly has been going on here at this facility?"

The man looked at her pleadingly. "It was sanctioned. By the office of the RP."

Evans responded first. "What was sanctioned?"

The doctor looked at Melissa. "The experiments. We have been working XRST. We neutralized it and enhanced it."

The revelation struck Melissa. "XRST? The virus that caused the Great Plague?"

"Yes. It was a project of mine that I have taken on from notes of previous researchers. We found we could use it to build super powerful soldiers."

"You've been testing it on the prisoners," Evans interjected.

"Yes! It enhanced their strength and their eyesight. Other benefits as well. But there were side effects. They became feral...like wild beasts. I have been working to tweak the formula. I was close."

"Close?" asked Melissa. "What was the purpose of this? We are not at war."

The doctor eyed her. "You'll have to ask the Regional President. She has grand plans. Particularly with the rabble in the Wildlands."

Melissa knew that the Gray Roses operated out of the Wildlands, but much of the population out there was neutral. They formed their own communities and townships. While she believed they dealt with the Gray Roses, and even harbored them occasionally, she did not think those communities were a great threat to the UGC. "You said that you were close. What did you mean by that?"

"They released the original creations into the Wildlands as a test. They sent some up near York, others to the west, around Frederick Town. They released still more to the east. This latest group. They were something special. They were better. While they were still uncontrollable, there was something to them. An intellect not seen in the first group."

"That doesn't sound close," said Evans. "That sounds like they are more dangerous."

"Yes. But I was working on the solution. Until…"

Melissa said, "Until tonight. What happened?"

"I was working in my office. There was a loud bang from below. That is when the power went out." He paused a moment. "I went back to my office. I secured the prototype I was working on." Melissa nodded to the officer who went into the office. The doctor continued. "Then I grabbed my tablet and began downloading my work to it. I grabbed the override tablet and came out to connect to the data. That is when she arrived."

"She?"

"The girl. She knocked me down. At first, I thought she was one of the terrorlings." Melissa realized she must have scrunched her face in confusion as the doctor said, "That is what the guards started calling the creatures. Anyway, though she was dressed differently, I recognized her. She had been working here for a few days now. She was a custodian.

John turned to Melissa. "One of the missing staff." He looked back at the doctor. "Julie Simmons?"

"That is the name that she gave. I suspect it is not her real name. She is a Gray Rose."

Melissa considered the information. "What makes you think that? Did she confirm it?"

"Well, she didn't deny it. She mentioned her sister. Apparently, she was a prisoner here."

"What happened to the girl?"

"She took the override tablet and left."

"There was a tablet found connected in the lobby," Evans chimed in.

Dr. Weaver shook his head. "She let them out, didn't she? They escaped the facility?"

At that moment, the door to the room opened. Melissa turned to see Michelle enter the room. "What is going on here? You assured me that these things were under control."

Melissa spoke up, "Michelle, we are in the middle of questioning the doctor."

The Warden stepped back. "This is my facility."

"And you knew about these experiments. We will be questioning you as well. I'm curious how such a secure facility could be breached by a terrorist."

Michelle looked aghast. "Oh, no! Don't put those things on me. I was against it from the beginning. But Dr. Weaver here has some special connections at HQ. I was told to allow him to perform his experiments with the prisoners. This disaster is all on him."

The officer who went into the office returned. He was carrying a lab coat in one hand and a piece of paper in the other. "Agent Davis, you should see this. It was in the doctor's lab coat." He handed her the paper. Melissa turned the paper over in her hands. Nobody used paper anymore. She looked at the doctor, who just shrank into himself.

"Doctor! Who is this message from?"

The doctor looked pale. "She was...my cousin, Rachel."

"What does she mean about associates?"

"I do not know! It is all rubbish."

Michelle spoke up incredulously. "Rachel? You told me she was dead! It's the Gray Roses, isn't it? You are responsible for all of this? Now, your monsters are out in the city."

Melissa spoke up. "Are you saying he is a traitor?"

Michelle shook her head. "No. He is just weak! He confided in me about his cousin a while ago. About how she had a *power* over him.

She would bat her eyes and he would do what she wanted. Supposedly she died. She jumped from a platform into the Undercity. But there was no body found. I suspected she was still alive, that she might be working with the Gray Roses.

The doctor sat there bristling. He was clearly becoming more agitated. "Agent Evans, take the Warden to another room; we will need to talk further."

Michelle went on. "You insufferable fool. I should have demanded that they send you elsewhere. I should have..." she cut off as her face twisted into horror. Evans, who was approaching to remove Michelle from the room, suddenly became animated as he reached down to draw his service weapon. A loud bang filled the room as blood and brain matter sprayed Evans and the wall behind him. Michelle crumbled to the floor. Melissa turned to the doctor, reaching for her own weapon. Smoke rose from the barrel of an old-fashioned gun. The doctor turned it and pointed it at his own temple. He pulled the trigger.

Click.

He pulled it again and again. *Click, click, click.* Finally, he lowered the weapon, dropping it to the floor. He sagged back in the chair as Evans and the guard moved in to take him into custody. The doctor began cackling as he resigned himself to the situation. It was going to be a long night.

Chapter Twenty

MEMORIES AND MEETINGS

2163.05.25 | 05:26

It was just as she remembered it. Only a bit more dust covered the floor and old furniture. The place had remained untouched for years. Rachel had been coming here every day now for the past several days. She was going to meet somebody here. With the chatter going on about a disturbance in the Essex District, she was almost certain that the meeting would be tonight.

When Rachel was younger, she frequented the Undercity. It was the one escape from the horrors of the world above.

She remembered the day she learned of the accident that claimed her parents. In a city where railbus crashes were unheard of, a freak accident took place. Her father was a prominent member of the UGC, a director in one of the many bureaucratic departments. She often heard him grumbling about what he did, what he had to do. What he was forced to do. Horrible decisions that haunted him throughout his life.

As a young child, there were moments when she stumbled upon him, tears streaming down his face. She would say nothing, just climb into his lap and hug him. He would hug her back and cry into her hair. When he calmed down, she would get up, give him a kiss, and go to bed and leave it at that. He never divulged what exactly it was that he did that upset him so. Just that he hated himself for it.

Rachel loved her father. When she was a little older, she overheard him talking to her mother about something that would change the way the world viewed the UGC if it were to get out. He knew things. It was a couple of days later when the accident happened.

The accident.

Rachel knew better. Something had happened. He got close to the truth, or he had it already. He was planning on revealing it. But he was stopped. Rachel was sent to live with her uncle, her mother's brother. He was rarely ever home, working a special job for the UGC that kept him away for long periods. Instead, she dealt with her aunt. That woman was truly devoted to the UGC. Who could blame her? They lived in a penthouse with plenty of room and quite a lot of luxury compared to most citizens. She spoiled her son, doting on him with all sorts of gifts. She let the boy have free rein and do whatever he wanted.

She remembered the boy, Alexander, taking a special interest in her. She caught him spying on her on more than one occasion. It got to where Rachel would indulge him. She would tease him. She honed that skill with the boy, learning how to manipulate him. It sickened her, but she knew it was how she was going to survive. She hated the UGC. And that was before they took her children.

Around the time that Alex left for his academy training, she was matched and married. She was still young. Perhaps it was a way to settle with her for the "loss" of her parents. Even though her husband was ten years her senior, she didn't mind the man. It got her away from her horrible aunt and absent uncle, at least. Perhaps, deep down, she even harbored some affection for her husband. She became pregnant and had twins. She loved them. When it was time for their testing, the officials showed some concern. She didn't have a choice. Her children were terminated.

Rachel stopped caring. Her husband escaped her grief with his work. She found an access point to the Undercity and sought solitude there. That was where she met Joe, a charming rogue from the Wildlands who often hid out in the Undercity. They became fast friends. He offered her a chance to escape from her life, and she took it. She staged her suicide and leaped off a platform into the Undercity. Of course, Joe had arranged for her safe landing, but the demonstration convinced onlookers she killed herself. It was enough. The UGC logged her death as such, thanks to contacts provided by Joe.

Her mind returned to the present. The fool had gotten himself captured. He was always so cavalier. She supposed that there wasn't much that he could do to avoid it. At least they still had a window to mount a rescue. And with the news coming in from Essex District, if her hunches were correct, she expected the window may be extended. If only Jenna would get there to make her report.

He took her to the Wildlands and introduced her to some friends. Shortly after that, the group of them formed what would become known as the Gray Roses. Their goal was to bring down the UGC.

Rachel walked through the old, abandoned house as she reminisced. During the early days, she would stay there whenever she needed to lay low and remain hidden. She was surprised one night to find two young girls staying there. She learned that the mother who left them there was dead. Rachel took those girls under her wing and fell in love with them. They became like her own daughters.

With care and dedication, she simultaneously raised and prepared them for the path they were destined to follow. She had no doubt of their strength, but she was feeling empty inside. Jenna, the younger one, was the source of her worry. She looked out the window. In the Undercity house, the absence of a visible sky didn't stop her from sensing the gradual lightening of the surroundings as dawn arrived.

As she looked out, her mind drifted to that of another girl, one she met just recently. Rachel's contacts found more information about that girl. Her test date was later this morning. There was something about her. Rachel could not let her fall victim to the UGC. She just got the acknowledgement from the testing official. All she could do was wait and see what happened.

A noise from inside the house pulled Rachel from her thoughts. She turned and cautiously walked to the door. The UGC did not come down here, but Rachel didn't survive without taking care. She heard a floorboard creaking in the lower level of the house. Following the sound, she smiled when she saw Jenna in the room where she and her sister took refuge all those years ago. "You took long enough, girl."

Jenna looked up, hardly surprised—but a bit relieved—to see Rachel. The girl rushed up to her, holding out the device. "Here, I retrieved the data."

Rachel was astonished by the mix of emotions she was reading from Jenna. Her face kept shifting from sorrow to fear to anger to relief in a rapid cycle. She reached out but did not take the drive. Instead, she gripped the girl's arm and pulled her into an embrace. Jenna sobbed softly into her shoulder. "What happened, child?"

Jenna relayed the details of the night. Rachel was astonished by the tale of the creatures, and that Kara was one of them. The news infuriated her. When Jenna informed Rachel about her run-ins with Alex, she could not hide a grimace. She could not tell whether she hated or pitied the man, but if he was responsible for these creatures, tales of which she had heard from the Wildlands, then right now she loathed him.

When Jenna mentioned Spencer, she contemplated his involvement. "I do not know of him. We had no other operatives besides you in that facility. The man is likely a loner. It happens from time to time. People acting on their own against the UGC because they are fed up with the practices. I will make an inquiry about him. If he still lives, it might be good if we find him."

Jenna nodded. She slumped down on an old couch. A dust cloud exploded into the air as she did, but the girl mostly ignored it, waving a hand as she leaned back.

Rachel looked at the data device. She desperately hoped that it had what they were looking for. She looked back at Jenna and firmed up. "Don't get too comfortable, young lady. We have much work to do."

"What is going on?"

"Joe has been taken by the UGC." Jenna's eyes opened wide, and she looked as though her breath was trapped in her lungs. "The news just reached me. They took him during a surprise ambush in Annapolis District. He was on a recruiting drive. The recruit was a disgruntled worker at the shipping yard, but it turned out to be a well-crafted sting. PPU agents jumped out and surrounded Joe."

Jenna stood up. She began adjusting her outfit as if she were ready to rush out right then and there. "If we lose Joe, that would be a mighty blow against us. It may even counter any victory we scored tonight."

Rachel held up a hand. "Relax, child! You are right. It would be devastating. That is where you will come in. I know you've had a long night, but we can't hesitate."

"I'm ready to do whatever I have to do. I already lost Kara. I can't lose Uncle Joe, too."

Rachel smiled at the affectionate title. Of course, Joe wasn't really the girl's uncle, but he acted like one toward her. Rachel found it interesting that she didn't call Mitch by the title. "Very good! Thanks to whatever went down at the facility, they are going to transport him to Philadelphia. They can't risk air transport, so they are going to go via railbus."

"Where do I get on?"

"Silver Spring...at the Testing Center."

"The Testing Center? Why there?"

Rachel smiled. She began weaving a tale about a little girl who thought a folded paper tossed into the wind was a butterfly.

Chapter Twenty-One

WELCOMED NEWS

2163.05.25 | 06:05

"Go on back," instructed Evans. "I'll catch a rail from here." The pilot of the transport acknowledged.

Melissa stopped at the edge of the rooftop landing pad as Evans caught up to her. They both watched as the transport rose and crossed the sky, now glowing amber in the eastern half edge. After a moment, Melissa moved on to the access door. Evans followed her into the building.

"Thanks for doing this. Tina would be upset if I arrived home with blood on me."

Melissa shook her head. "I wouldn't blame her. Come on. I am certain Darren won't mind you borrowing a shirt. I pinged him about it on the way."

She led him down the stairs. It had been a long night at the facility. The doctor was taken back to the PPU headquarters for temporary holding. A relief team finally arrived so that Melissa and Evans could get some much-needed sleep.

On the third landing, she entered the main corridor. Evans spoke up as they walked down the hall. "What do you think about our mystery girl?"

Melissa didn't hesitate. "She is definitely a Rose!"

"My thinking, too. How many regular citizens do you think could get a hold of a scrambler?" He chuckled at his own thought. "And her 'supervisor?' This Spencer...Do you think she recruited him?"

"That could be the case, but I don't know. My gut tells me maybe not. The cameras showed that he just walked into the power station with barely a care. And the footage of him after the explosion when he exited the prison section...he seemed different. He was—"

"Elated!" Evans finished for her. She nodded. "Four police bots! She took out four of them."

"You almost sound like you admire her!" Melissa said as she pressed her thumb to the access panel of her apartment.

"I do...in a way. At least, I am impressed."

Melissa smiled as she opened the door. Evans followed. It was a nicely sized apartment given her station. It was enough for her and Darren with room to expand. She called out, "Darren! Are you here? Did you get my ping?"

A voice came from the back room. "Coming out now." Darren entered the room carrying a shirt. He wasn't wearing anything at all, and Melissa cracked a smile as she felt herself blush. She looked at her partner. If her cheeks were burning, then Evans' cheeks were on fire. He stuttered a thanks to Darren for the shirt, then left the room to change.

She shook her head. "I can't believe you!" She tried to appear upset, but the crack in her voice showed otherwise.

"What? I have been waiting for you for a long time. He's lucky I didn't jump you as soon as you walked in the door." He smiled as he went into the kitchen and poured them both some seltzer. "I have news for you." He handed her a cup.

She took the cup and her face turned hopeful. "Was it successful?"

His smile gave the answer away before he even said anything. "The doctor confirmed it. The surrogate is five weeks."

Melissa placed the cup down and embraced her husband. "That's wonderful." She kissed him deeply as he pulled her in. Since they were matched, he'd always wanted to be a father. But Melissa's job was on a higher level, so he would be the one to stay home with the child. They had to go with a surrogate because of her line of work.

Darren pulled off her jacket and started to untuck her shirt as he backed her to the couch. She could feel him getting excited. She reached up and brushed his beard. "When are you going to get rid of this thing?"

His smile was sly. "Never! I love the way you squirm when it tickles you." He slipped his hand to her side and started poking at her. She chuckled at the tickle, but grabbed him in a hug, pulling him into her. The move caused her to fall back along the couch, pulling Darren with her.

As he slipped a hand up her shirt to grip her breast, they heard a throat clearing. Melissa looked over and saw Evans standing there, trying not to look. Darren, not moving from pinning Melissa down, looked over at him and said, "Would you like to join us?"

Evan's eyes grew large in shock. "No...NO! I...should be leaving. I must get home to Tina."

Melissa laughed. "John, Darren's just joking! We just received some great news. We are going to have a child.

"Congratulations! But I DO have to go." He gave an awkward smile. "You two have a head start, but I've got Tina waiting for me. Give it an hour, you might hear her. I'll see myself out. You have fun."

He laughed as he left, his attempt to defuse the situation falling a bit flat.

Melissa looked up at her husband, who smiled down at her. "I can't believe it," he said. "We are finally going to have a child."

She reached up and brushed his cheek. His smile grew deeper at the touch. "I know you are going to be a great father." For a moment, the events of the night flooded her brain. The horror that welcomed her at the facility, the questioning of the doctor. The revelation of the creatures and watching the warden killed right in front of her all flashed in her head as if reminding her of the growing dangers.

Darren looked at her, his face twisting in concern. "What is the matter? Did something happen? Why DID your partner have blood on his shirt?"

"No need to worry. There was just an accident. As far as what is the matter...you know I don't like this position." In a swift motion, she grabbed his arm, twisted it, then flipped her husband off the couch and onto the floor. She rolled and landed, straddling him. He groaned in pain, but smiled with excitement. "That's better." She smiled.

Darren groaned. "That hurt! I landed on my shoulder!"

"I guess I'll have to make it up to you." She pulled her shirt off and leaned down to kiss him deeply.

Chapter Twenty-Two

THE TESTING

2163.05.25 | 10:00

"Mr. and Mrs. Hardin, we are ready for your daughter." Brett looked up to see the people standing in front of him. He glanced over at his wife, then motioned for his daughter to follow him. "Please wait here in the lobby," said the lab-coated official. "For the first part of the test, she will be alone. We will bring you into the observation deck for part two."

Brett nodded. "Go on, Olivia!" he said with a smile. "These people will talk with you for a bit. We will be with you again shortly."

Olivia followed the two proctors. After they disappeared through the doors, he returned to Lindsey and Scott. Lindsey took his hand as he sat beside her. She had a smile on her face. He smiled back, though he had to force it. Despite how wonderful he felt the night before, he couldn't help but feel nervous. Lindsey must have felt his tension, and she squeezed his hand.

A video display on the wall was relaying the daily news. Brett tried to listen to the report to distract his thoughts, but he couldn't stop his mind from jumping to his daughter, and that allowed only parcels of information from the broadcast through. He heard something about a disaster at the Containment Facility in the Northeast quarter of the Capital Metro that caused the death of several workers. There was also news that the notorious terrorist known as Giuseppe Valentino, leader of the Gray Roses, had been captured and was undergoing interrogation.

Normally, Brett would be absorbing those stories, but his mind kept drifting. The night before, he felt so happy. Olivia was doing great with her studies. Then he reflected on the previous week. The news of the facility accident conjured up thoughts of Eric Larson. His former coworker likely would have been at the facility. Brett couldn't explain the sting of pain when he thought about Eric being hurt in the disaster. He never really knew him that well. He supposed it didn't really matter.

At the present, the only thing that really mattered to Brett was his family. Olivia was facing the most important test in her life...a test that would measure her on several factors. It would determine the level of career they would assign her and dictate the training she would receive for the rest of her childhood.

Brett considered the possible tiers that they could place her in. He was confident that the lowest two tiers could be crossed off. The lowest was reserved for menial, often dangerous jobs like mining, cleaning, or Undercity maintenance. Those jobs were often done by robots unless they felt a human was better suited. The next tier up was the basic working class. Factory support, advanced maintenance, and even low-end PPU guards fell into that tier.

Brett and Lindsey were in the lower-middle tier. Before the children were born, Lindsey worked with him at the same office. She was a data interpreter. She collected the data that Brett would input into the database. Right now, she was on an extended break. Once Scott was placed into job training, she would return to the job originally assigned.

Brett watched as Lindsey tended to their son. Scott did not show the same level of aptitude as Olivia. If anything, he was average. That was fine. Much like Lindsey and Brett, Scott would score a menial but important job. Olivia, on the other hand, was destined for greatness. She could be a top member of the UGC, maybe even the Regional President. This was one of very few chances to rise in status in the UGC. Olivia certainly had the intelligence for it. No. Brett was not concerned about her aptitude.

"We have to trust in her." Brett stirred from his thoughts as he heard Lindsey speak. He looked up at her, the smile on her face warming his heart. It was comforting. He looked at his son, Scott, and ruffled his head.

"I hope so!" Brett replied. "I only want the best for her."

"As do we all." They remained there in silence for what seemed an eternity, though Brett supposed it was only about an hour.

Finally, an administrator came out to meet them and bid them to follow. They were taken to a dark room where they could observe their daughter as she continued with the next phase of her test. She was sitting on the floor, a myriad of toys and puzzles surrounding her. The proctors stood to the side, a dark-skinned man and a woman with copper-red hair. They observed her actions as she manipulated the toys. Occasionally, they would ask her questions about what she was doing. Brett smiled as Olivia solved the puzzles with ease.

Then, the male proctor asked Olivia, "What do you dream about?" Brett was confused. He looked at Lindsey, who was equally surprised by the question.

"A lot of things!" came the soft yet delighted response.

"Can you specify? What dreams bring you happiness?" Brett was growing concerned by the line of questioning. Something was not right.

Olivia smiled. "Rainbows...and butterflies, too!"

The female proctor asked, "Why do those bring you happiness?"

"Because they are beautiful, silly!" The male proctor nodded; his expression was grim. The female proctor tapped furiously at her tablet.

Brett closed his mind to the questioning. He had heard enough. After a few more questions, the viewing window went dark. The administrator motioned to a table in the room. "Please take a seat. The proctors will be with you shortly." Brett forgot the administrator was still in the room with them.

Thoughts raced through his head. His gut ached, and so did his mind. "I love her!" He put his head into his hands. "What are we going to do?"

"I don't know!" came Lindsey's response in a voice just as shaky as his own. "We must believe that things will work out. Maybe they will overlook her responses." Brett could hear in her voice that she didn't really believe her own words. He watched her as she hugged Scott close to her chest.

Time moved on as they sat there; Brett did not know how much. Finally, the door opened, and the two proctors came in. Grim expressions on their faces confirmed the worst. The male proctor flashed what Brett perceived as a sympathetic smile. The badge over the left breast of his uniform read *John Dalton*. He spoke up first. "Olivia is a very intelligent little girl." The assurance did not mute the dread in Brett's heart.

The female proctor, whose badge named her *Lori Bartlet,* continued the assessment. "She passed all her academics with top grades. You did well in preparing her. That, in itself, would be very fortunate." Brett braced his emotions as she continued. "However, we regret that her personality tests did not meet UGC standards. She fell short in the categories of Realism and Conformity."

Lindsey was shocked. "Realism and Conformity? I don't understand. There was no reference to those categories in the training material."

Proctor Bartlet replied, "They are new categories, added after we sent the materials out. It does not matter because they deal more in the abstract nature of the personality. Her high aptitude and her lack of grip on reality are a very dangerous combination. It is my opinion that she be set for immediate termination."

"Termination?" Both Brett and Lindsey nearly said it at the same time with such ferocity that Scott started crying. Lindsey tried to hush him as Brett said again, "Termination? How? I can't even fathom..."

Proctor Dalton again flashed that sympathetic smile. "Mr. and Mrs. Hardin. Please try to remain calm. There are alternatives that can be pursued."

Lindsey perked up. "What alternatives?" she asked. "How can we help our daughter?"

"As my colleague mentioned, termination is one option. It is done quickly and painlessly, and you would be rewarded 50,000 credits and given authorization for a *third*."

Brett felt wetness on his cheek as he shook his head. He looked at Lindsey. "What are the alternatives?"

"There is a special rehab facility in Philadelphia that can remove undesirable traits. It would need to be done immediately. There, she will undergo extensive conditioning. It had been quite a successful process, though it has its downfalls."

"What downfalls?" Lindsey responded.

Proctor Bartlet took over. "She will remain in the facility for at least a year, at the end of which she will be tested again. If there is any progress, she will continue until she is certified for placement."

"If she does not show improvement, or a period of five years passes without her being certified, she will be automatically assigned for termination," Dalton continued. "At which point we will reward the provisions mentioned earlier." He paused for a moment to let them take it in. "On the other hand, when she *does* pass, she will be behind her fellow students. She has an advantage with her high aptitude. But there is a chance that the treatment could bring that down."

Lindsey and Brett looked at each other. Lindsey's eyes were wet, and Brett could feel tears running down his own cheeks. Bartlet resumed. "You should understand...the high aptitude that your daughter displays, along with her 'dreaminess' and non-conformity, are a dangerous combination. If unchecked, she will be susceptible to corruption and a danger to society."

Brett and Lindsey sat there in silence for a time. The only sound in the room was an occasional coo from Scott that brought smiles to the faces of the proctors. Brett turned to them, his voice empty and hoarse. "I suppose we have only one option. We cannot give up on her so easily."

Bartlet smiled. "Very well! And as we expected. We have already booked her for enrollment at the Philadelphia Rehab Center. It will be difficult, but they have the highest rate of rehabilitation. You will be allowed to accompany her to the facility and attend her orientation into the program. There, you can say your goodbyes. We will make arrangements with your office, Mr. Hardin. The railbus will be on the platform soon, so you can make your way there. Olivia will be waiting for you. Best of luck to you." She turned and left the room.

Proctor Dalton motioned for them to follow and led them back to the building's lobby. Producing a railbus card, he handed it over to Brett, then placed an arm on Brett's shoulder. "Mr. and Mrs. Hardin, opportunities can appear when you don't expect them to. I suggest you take them." Brett was confused. The man nodded toward the front door. "Your daughter should be at the platform now." He left them standing in the lobby.

Brett turned to his wife. He could tell that she was not having an easy time letting go of her anger. "Come! Let's go to our daughter." Lindsey looked at him and some of the anger washed out of her face. She took his hand as they crossed the lobby to the door.

CHAPTER TWENTY-THREE

THE RAILBUS

2163.05.25 | 11:15

A light breeze swept across the walkway as Brett, Lindsey, and Scott crossed it to the boarding station. Olivia was already there, accompanied by two attendants from the Center. As soon as she saw them, she started running for them. Brett reached out and lifted her into a tight embrace as Olivia jumped into his arms. "They told me I have to go to a special school far away," she said. He stood there hugging her for several moments before finally putting her down.

While Olivia went over to hug Lindsey and Scott, Brett turned to the custodians. One handed him a card. "The bus will be here in a few minutes. This card is your pass, four to the Philadelphia Rehab Center, three to return to your home station."

Brett took the card and the two custodians left without another word, leaving the family almost alone. One other person stood on the platform, a woman of an age close to his own, maybe a little younger.

As promised, the railbus arrived in short order. Brett guided his family onto the bus, following the woman. It was not crowded, but the passengers surprised him a bit. The bus had a conductor, which was unusual. The dark blonde man smiled at them as he motioned them to a seat. Besides the solitary woman that boarded with them, there was a couple about ten years older than Brett and Lindsey sitting across from each other. The couple contrasted each other in looks and demeanor. The man stared at a tablet, not even acknowledging that anybody else was there. Brett wondered if the two were even a couple. They seemed so different. More curiously, there was a man bound in restraints and wearing an eye blocker, flanked by two PPU agents. Brett was confused. Why would a prisoner be on the railbus? He wondered if it had anything to do with the accident at the containment facility that he saw on the newsreel earlier.

The conductor announced, "Welcome! Please hold your youngest in your lap while we are in motion." Lindsey nodded, and they chose a section of four seats, two facing the others, near the front of the bus. Brett sat in one of the rear-facing seats with Olivia next to him. Lindsey took the seat across from him, holding onto Scott.

Once everyone was seated, the conductor announced, "We will now make our way to Philadelphia Metro. Please remain seated for the duration of the trip. Now departing Testing Center, Silver Spring." He pressed a button on the console and the railbus began moving. This railbus would leave the metro and traveled through the Wildlands.

The conductor called out, "We are now transitioning to the main rail. Please remain seated." The main rail was at a higher level than the local railways, so the railbus had to go up a steep incline. The railbus leveled out next to the main rail before merging onto it. As it did, the railbus's speed increased rapidly. The windows darkened to lessen the blur of the city moving past. As the transition occurred, Brett put his hand on Olivia. She was looking out the window in amazement. "I love you, Olivia."

She looked up at him and smiled. "I love you, too, Daddy. Don't worry! Everything will be okay." Brett barely heard Lindsey choke up as he fought back tears himself. He reached over and gave Olivia a big hug.

"She is lovely!" came the voice from across the aisle. Brett and Lindsey both turned to regard the woman across from them. "Thank you!" they said, nearly in unison.

"I'm sorry about your situation," she continued. Brett examined the lady. He was certain that she was at least ten years older, but he would almost place her near retirement age. Her blonde hair had streaks of silver and lines marked her forehead and under her eyes. The man that sat across from her had lines on his face that mirrored the woman's and a hairline far back on his head. He seemed lost in his own world, his head buried in the device he held. "I felt the same way two years ago when my Kyle was sent to the Center. He hasn't been certified yet, but one more year should do it. You know we get to visit them on their anniversaries, right?"

"No, they didn't mention that." Lindsey was rather interested in the lady now. "I am Lindsey—this is my husband, Brett, and our children, Olivia and Scott."

The lady smiled. "My name is Debra. The Center really works wonders. Kyle was very special. When he came of age, he was light-years beyond anybody else. That seems to be happening more and more of late. Perhaps whatever they are putting in the baby food is working wonders." She chuckled, and Brett heard a scoff. He assumed it came from the man across from her. Debra went on as if she didn't hear. "But he had certain traits that caused great concern. Sadly, that often seems to be the case for the highly intelligent. We were offered the choice. We chose the right one. I am certain. Isn't that right, love?"

The man finally looked up at Brett and his family. "If you ask me, it wasn't much of a choice." He turned back to his device and disengaged from the conversation again. Brett and Lindsey looked at each other. He could see the concern creeping into her face.

"Don't mind Stan," Debra continued. "He took it hard. But we will get through this — I know we will." As quickly as that, she went back to her own device and remained silent.

Brett gave Lindsey a questioning look. She shrugged. From the corner of his eye, he saw the other female passenger was staring at Olivia. When he glanced her way, he could see the sympathy on her face. She saw him, gave a comforting smile, then looked away. He turned back to Lindsey. "We *DID* make the right decision," he affirmed in a low voice.

He looked up at the tracker that showed where the railbus was. They were going through Baltimore District. He scooped Olivia up and placed her on his lap, then motioned to Lindsey. She got up and moved to the seat beside him, and the four embraced as the bus rocketed along the rail.

Silence filled the bus as it continued along. Before too long, it slowed a bit as they approached the city limit. Brett looked out the window and could see the city wall approaching. Within moments, blackness engulfed them. He looked around at the other passengers, who seemed unaffected by the sudden change. In a matter of seconds, the daylight returned, and he could see the wall behind them. The conductor announced, "We are now in the Wildlands. Please remain vigilant." Brett hugged his family close while the bus, again, picked up speed.

Olivia looked amazed as she peered out the window. Within moments, the bus was running beside trees. Some came close to the platform. Brett smiled at the wonderment in her eyes. "Do you think there will be any animals out here?" she asked.

Brett scanned the trees as they passed. "Perhaps. We will probably go too fast to see them."

Movement caught his eye, and he looked at the lone woman. She had pulled a strange device out of her pocket—it looked like a clunky remote of some kind. She fiddled with it as she looked out the window. Was she counting?

Suddenly, the railbus's interior lights went dark. The bus slammed onto the rail, throwing the passengers up in the air. Brett cradled his screaming family. A screeching squeal let out as the fail-safe brakes gripped the tracks. Gradually, the bus slowed and came to a stop. "Is everybody okay?" Brett asked.

"Yes...just a bit shaken." Scott cried in Lindsey's arms. She examined him, then pulled him in for a tight hug. "Scott looks okay; he is just scared."

"What happened, Daddy?" Olivia was looking around, her face horrified.

"I don't know!" Brett replied, as he looked over at the lady. She gave him a shrug. Stan appeared terrified, and Debra looked around in confusion. He then looked to the rear of the bus. One of the PPU guards was handling the man that Brett assumed to be a prisoner, while the other was fiddling with a comm device.

"We lost power!" The conductor's voice sounded troubled. "Our systems appear to be fried." Brett turned to look at the man. He saw him open a panel and fiddle with some switches.

"My comm is dead," the PPU guard shouted.

"Do not worry—I just deployed the distress signal. Help will arrive soon. Everybody, please remain calm and in your seats."

The passengers all settled in. Stan grumbled, "Oh...I can't use my tab."

"It's okay, dear," Debra responded in a cheery voice. "You can live without it for a bit. We'll get you a new one as soon as we get back."

"Daddy, everything will be okay, won't it?" Olivia asked.

Brett brushed her cheek. "Yes, it will. You don't have to be frightened."

She looked around the bus and settled her gaze out the window. "Now that we're stopped, maybe I'll get to see an animal."

Brett smiled at her. He stared out the window at a small craft approaching. "You see? Our rescue is here." He pointed as the craft flew over and aligned next to the bus. It was a UGC transport craft capable of carrying a load of people. While the conductor moved to open the bus door, a hatch opened, and a plank extended between the two vehicles. Two PPU officials dressed in full gear, including fatigues and visored helmets, boarded the railbus. One turned to speak to the conductor, the other looked to the rear of the bus. "Do you have full control of your prisoner?"

The first PPU guard nodded and turned to assist the other with the prisoner. A blast rang out, and an energy bolt struck the second guard, sending him slumping in the seat. As the first guard turned back, a second bolt struck him in the chest, sprawling him against the rear of the bus. The PPU soldier that fired the bolts ran back to the prisoner.

The lone woman stood up and raced back to the prisoner as well. "Joe!" she yelled as she and the armed guard worked on releasing his restraints.

"What...what is going on?" cried the conductor.

The other soldier—a woman, Brett realized—smiled as she pointed her weapon at the conductor. He backed up, raising his hands beside his head. The now freed prisoner addressed the group. "Hello! I apologize for the scare. As you probably have guessed by now, I am Giuseppe Valentino, and we are the Gray Roses. You have nothing to fear. My associates and I will depart now. You are welcome to join us. In fact, I encourage it. Whatever the case, we must hurry. If you choose, you can wait for the Cleaners to arrive. But I must warn you, it is dangerous here. Now, more dangerous than ever."

Lindsey looked at Brett, hope in her eyes. Brett was in shock. This was the fearsome Giuseppe Valentino? The man was certainly imposing with his large, muscular frame. He had a close haircut common among soldiers and guards. It all came together in Brett's mind...the woman, the device she carried, the false UGC soldiers. He looked at the woman. "You did this! You caused the railbus to stop."

"It had to be done." She glanced at Lindsey and Olivia. "Given your situation, you should probably be thankful. For the life of your precious little girl, I'd urge you to come with us."

Giuseppe cut in. "I agree with Jenna here. But, whatever you decide, we must hurry."

Brett hesitated. Everything was happening too fast. Thoughts went through his head rapidly. Memories of Eric Larson being arrested...the mysterious woman at the celebration... the man on the platform...Olivia's test. Finally, he remembered what the proctor had said.

"Opportunities can show up when you don't expect them to. I suggest you take them."

Lindsey was standing with Scott in one arm, holding on to Olivia's hand with the other. Brett saw the conflict in her eyes. Sorrow and anger. Pleading yet daring. He put an arm around her, then took Olivia's hand. "Let's go!"

The others were already on the transport. Stan was guiding Debra, who seemed excited, across the plank. The female soldier and Giuseppe were at the door. Brett scooped up Olivia and guided his family to the door. Brett looked at the plank and the ground below. "Just run across. You'll be fine," Giuseppe said. Brett gripped his daughter tightly in his arms and moved forward. He skidded to a halt and turned as Lindsey followed on his heels.

Jenna aided Lindsey with the children while Brett turned toward the door. He held out a hand as the last soldier ran across the plank. He did the same for Giuseppe, pulling him into the transport. The conductor was at the door of the railbus. "You are all crazy."

Giuseppe yelled to him, "If you are staying, step back, sir."

The conductor looked torn. Movement from atop the railbus caught Brett's eye. The silhouette of a figure rose and stood there. Giuseppe yelled, "Shit! We MUST go now!" He caught a gun that was tossed to him by one of the fake guards. and turned toward the figure. Brett heard him said under his breath, "I was afraid we would attract them." Another figure was rising beside the first.

A loud screech filled the air as the first leaped down onto the plank, revealing its monstrous form. Giuseppe fired his gun at the creature, but the shots barely affected it. It hissed and ran into the railbus. The conductor yelled out as the plank came free, and Giuseppe pulled the handle on the hatch. Brett could hear the horrible screams of the conductor and saw the second creature leaping toward the transport as the door closed.

A thud sounded against the hull of the craft, and Brett heard the thing screeching as it clung to the transport. The craft was moving away from the rail and gaining speed. Giuseppe ran up to the pilot's cabin. "That thing is hanging on to the outside."

"I'll take care of it," the pilot responded. He pressed a button, and arcs of blue enveloped the outside of the vessel. A scream erupted outside the cabin and faded away. "Threat eliminated!"

Brett stood up. "What *WAS* that thing?"

"That was the work of the UGC," said Jenna. "They created those things and released them on the free people."

"Free people?"

"Yes, the free people," Giuseppe answered. "Those of us who live outside of and unbound by UGC society and rules. The people shut out from the cities."

Before Brett could ask another question, an alarm sounded. "We're losing fuel," said the pilot. "That thing must have punctured the tank. We must put her down. Brace for a hard landing." Brett moved over to his family. The craft descended rapidly. Brett gripped his family tight. "Impact in three...two...one..." The craft jolted as it struck the ground. Scott started crying. The momentum of the craft bounced the passengers around. Brett heard a thump and saw Stan lying on the floor of the craft. Brett held on with all he could. Finally, the transport came to a stop.

CHAPTER TWENTY-FOUR

THE WILDLANDS

2163.05.25 | 11:57

There was a hissing sound interlaced by the crackling of small fires. Brett slowly sat up, loosening his grip on his family. "Anybody hurt?"

Lindsey began inspecting the children. "I think we're good."

Giuseppe was on his feet in a moment. He walked past Brett and patted him on the shoulder. "You've got some strong and brave kids." He went to a cabinet in the transport's rear. Stan got up, moaning. Giuseppe returned with some rifles and began handing them out.

As he handed one to Stan, Debra said, "I just want to see my Kyle."

"Kyle's dead, you nut!" Stan said, irritably. "As good as, anyway."

"How can you say that? He's our everything!"

"He's nothing like he was. They turned him into...a...something. They removed his soul." He turned to Brett. "If you ask me, this is the best thing that could have happened to your family."

Giuseppe stepped in front of Brett and handed him a rifle. He pulled a pistol from his belt and handed it to Lindsey. "You're gonna have your hands full with your kids, but I'm not leaving anybody without the means to defend themselves. Keep this secure. We'll do our best to cover you. The most important thing is to keep up." He turned to the soldiers. "Jim, Sara, Mark...head out and secure the area. We'll be out shortly. What's the status, Jack?"

"I've got our coordinates," the pilot responded as the other uniformed soldiers left the transport. "We head southeast for a half-mile, and we'll be on the road to Elk. We've got some vehicles stored away that will get us to the school."

"Roger that! All right, people. Let's head out. We've gotta move fast if we're gonna stay ahead of those creatures."

Giuseppe stood by the hatch while the rest filed out of the craft. Sparse trees surrounded them. Strange sounds echoed through the crash site. Giuseppe came out and brought a long sling over to Brett. He tied the ends to each of Brett's shoulders and placed Olivia in the sling. "Hold on tight to your dad, little one. That should help you. We need to move fast, and I don't intend to leave anyone behind."

"Thank you. You're not what I imagined...uh...Mr. Valentino."

Giuseppe smiled. "Call me Joe." He turned to the pilot. "Give the word."

"That way! The old road should be just over the hill." Distant screams echoed through the trees.

"That's our cue. Let's move out!"

They began a brisk walk. Brett looked toward Lindsey and found that she was also wearing a sling to hold Scott, only hers was in the front where she could hug him close as they moved. Brett found the sling really helped with Olivia's added weight on his back. "Hold tight, Olivia girl."

After a few minutes of walking, they heard the screams again, still distant, but clearly closer. They crested the hill and could see the road. Momentum gathered as they rushed toward it. The screams continued behind them. Brett moved alongside Giuseppe...Joe. "What is Elk?"

"Elkton! It is a town, long abandoned. Many of the free peoples have gathered in abandoned towns in the Wildlands. Some, like Elk, remain empty. We know this one well. We have old vehicles and supplies stored there."

"And *the school*?"

Joe glanced at him. "It's what it says...an old school. The old campus of the University of Delaware. It has become one of our major outposts. We make it there, and we'll be safe...at least for a time. I reckon the UGC will want to retaliate and will home in on us eventually. Be we can worry about that once we reach the school." He looked ahead. "Remain alert."

Once they stepped foot on the pavement of the road, a scream filled the air. It was close. They broke into a run. One soldier at the rear turned. Brett looked back as a creature emerged from the trees in a full-on run. With precision, the soldier directed his weapon and pulled the trigger. The first bolt hit, then the second. The creature didn't stumble. A third struck its head, but it was too late. It dove onto the soldier, and Brett heard his screams as it tore into him. "Don't look back!" came a shout as something flew back toward the creature. Brett faced the road ahead and quickened his pace. He heard a pop from behind and saw the residual flash of light at the edges of his eyesight, followed by the creature's screaming.

Lindsey ran up beside him, clutching Scott close. He felt Olivia's grip tighten on his shoulders. Carefully holding the rifle in one hand, he took Lindsey's hand with the other.

Soon, the first buildings of the town came into view. Vines wrapped around many of them, parts of the structures crumbling from their embrace. Joe and Jenna led them through winding roads to a building with a faded sign that read *Frank's Autobody*. Joe ushered the group in. Once they were all inside, he closed and locked the door behind them.

***

"The backup of the data is complete." Rachel sat back in her chair. She stared at the terminal, her mind racing through the information.

"Rachel?"

She turned to the source of the voice. Paul stood looking at her, the stubble on his face making him look like he was in shadow. She blinked. "Yes. Begin making copies immediately. We need to distribute it to all our outposts up and down the coast. I want Mitch to have a copy by tonight." She stood up and walked to a nearby window as Paul began carrying out her ordered. She looked out at the landscape, past the buildings and to the trees beyond. "Susan, any word on Joe?"

"We have reports that the railbus was stopped. We are trying to verify the status." Susan was young, in her mid-teens. She tied her ash-blonde hair into pigtails, which accentuated her youth. But her skills contrasted with that appearance. She acted as Rachel's assistant at the school and managed it while she was away. "We have confirmation that the girl was on the bus, along with her family. If you don't mind me asking, why is she important?"

Rachel closed her eyes. When she opened them again, she said, "Because she sees things like few other citizens of the UGC. Not only is she intelligent, but her imagination is also very active. She could be of great use to us. For decades, the UGC has been bent on crushing any free thought in its citizens. They want to have complete control. This girl is a defiance to that notion. With our guidance, she could rise to great importance and play a vital role in the liberation from the United Global Coalition."

Susan wrinkled her brow. "But why her? We have a lot of intelligent and creative people throughout the Wildlands."

"Because, child, that girl has a spark that I have never seen before. I don't know where my feelings come from. Are they prophecy or just intuition? In the end, it doesn't matter. She can see things like few others. The UGC view this as a threat, and that makes her an asset. Besides, not too long ago, you were slated for a similar fate, and I extracted you. I haven't regretted it one bit."

Susan beamed at that last remark. Rachel meant it. The girl had been a remarkable addition to their faction. She could see that Susan was considering what she said. "I will go see what we can find out." The girl left the room. Rachel resumed staring out the window. She whispered a prayer for Joe to arrive at the school with the child.

Paul walked up to her. "Here is the first copy. I have several more in progress." He handed her a data stick that she gladly took.

"Thank you, Paul. Do you think I am crazy?"

"Not at all. I know you. You have a gift for reading people. Whatever you saw in this *girl*...well, I trust she will live up to what you say."

Rachel thanked him again, then went to her office. The room used to belong to a professor back when the school was operational. Back before the virus. She left it as it was when she took over. She knew very little about the professor. They were long dead and forgotten. They were insignificant. But they had lived. That mattered. Where the UGC erased anything that didn't have to do with them, she wanted to hold on. Maybe one day, that professor's story could be told.

She sat at her terminal and plugged in the device. She pressed the button and waited for the terminal to power up.

After her meeting with Jenna early that morning, she immediately made her way to Annapolis District. Within an hour, she was out of the city and on a boat traveling up the bay. When it pulled into the old port at the mouth of the Susquehanna, she met with her contacts and rushed to the school to analyze the recovered data.

It didn't take long for Paul to crack into the files. She had pored over the information. Both Paul and Susan gasped repeatedly as they took it all in. Rachel held her composure, though. She had suspected much of the information the whole time. Some claimed that the virus that caused the Great Plague was manmade. This confirmed it. But it did more than that—it connected the virus to the founders of the UGC.

Rachel pulled the information up on her terminal and went through the files. Some were recent, others were as old as the UGC itself. The UGC appeared to be preparing satellites for launch, something that hadn't happened since before the Plague. The schematics of the new ones were far superior to the best technology available back then. This could be a problem for the Gray Roses.

It was something that they would have to deal with. First things first. They had to work on getting the news of the virus to the citizenry of the UGC. She was sure that they would counter it, but they wouldn't be able to stop the seed from taking root in the minds of the people. It was going to be a long fight. Rachel knew she might not live to see the end of it. But her proteges like Jenna and Susan, and with luck, that amazing girl...they could change the tide.

A knock at the door pulled her from her thoughts. "Come in."

Susan rushed in. "Rachel! We have news, but it's not good."

Rachel froze in her seat. "What is it?"

"The transport went down close to where the railbus was stopped. We're readying a team."

Rachel's heart sank. "Joe!" It had also hit her that Jenna would have been on the transport, too. She knew they were capable, though. "Don't send a rescue team. Deploy a drone. We need to find out if they survived the crash. Be ready. If they DID survive, and I have little doubt, Joe and Jenna can bring them in. They are our best operatives, and I don't want to risk more lives. Plus, a rescue team could draw unwanted attention from the UGC."

Susan nodded her understanding and left the room. Rachel stood up and went to the small window of the office. "Come on, Joe. Bring them in safely," she whispered.

CHAPTER TWENTY-FIVE

A REPRIEVE

2163.05.25 | 12:25

Joe turned to the group of refugees. "Everyone, take some time to rest and regroup. We have to get the vehicles ready, so we'll be here for a bit."

Joe, Jenna, the pilot, and the other soldiers moved to a couple of old vehicles that were in the garage. The two soldiers grabbed cans from a shelf and began fueling. Joe jumped in the larger vehicle, a pickup truck, while the pilot entered the smaller one. Brett put Olivia down and headed over to Stan. "What did you mean your son was dead?"

Stan looked at him, at first with disgust, but his face quickly softened to sympathy. "He's no longer my son. They changed him. He's still smart, but he has no emotion. To me, he's dead."

Jenna walked up to them at that moment. She regarded Brett. "That center you were taking your daughter to; it wasn't just some place to break habits. They *reprogram* people. Warp their minds. Your daughter, I suppose she is very intelligent, given her age? Does she like to play, not just with her 'assigned' toys, but with her mind?"

Brett nodded.

"They'd remove that from her. They like nothing to do with creativity—when combined with intelligence, they regard it as a threat. People may get *ideas*."

Brett chewed on the word. "Ideas?"

"An intelligent person is good if they follow along. But creative people look at things differently. They see things that others do not. They become a threat. Those that hold the power in the UGC, they are wary of anybody that might see through their designs."

"The UGC takes care of its citizens. Why would anybody want to change that?"

"Because they only take care of the citizens as long as they are useful. You are not really people to them, just tools. Somebody who can think beyond what they are told would be dangerous. They could expose them for what they really are."

Brett sat there, considering. Stan added, "You must realize... Debra and I weren't on our way to visit our son. He returned last year. Now he is in his career training. We were going to admit Debra to the place. She has lost her mind. They stole my son's soul and destroyed my wife's mind. As frightening as they are, I would rather deal with those monsters outside than with the monsters within the UGC. I am *done* with them."

Brett took it all in. He looked at Lindsey, who was sitting nearby, tending to Scott. From the intense look on her face, she clearly heard every word of the conversation. He couldn't believe everything. He'd lived his whole life doing his part for society—simply doing his assigned job and raising his family. The UGC provided everything he needed. But now, they wanted to take something away without regard for his feelings. What Jenna and Stan were saying hit home.

Now he wondered...were the fairy books a mistake? Or was blindly following the UGC the mistake?

He considered the monsters. They were horrifying. "Those...things? What are they? You said that they were created?"

Jenna looked wistfully into the distance. "The UGC calls them 'terrorlings.' They were once people, some of them former Roses, many just average citizens that stepped out of line. The prison created them. A pet project of the doctor there. Whatever the intent, the results were these mindless beasts of great strength. You've seen how hard they are to take down."

"Why would the UGC make them?"

"Who's to say? From what I could determine, they were trying to make super soldiers. They want to take back the Wildlands."

Lindsey spoke up. "Why are they even bothering with the Wildlands? What is the point?"

"Many reasons. When the UGC was founded, the population was a lot smaller. But since then, the population has been booming. Look at Capital Metro. Fifty years ago, the three separate Metros merged to create it. Nearly every space within the immense area is filling up quickly, even with the birth restriction mandate."

"The resources of the UGC are thinning out in the Metros. But the Wildlands are vast and ripe for expansion. There is just one thing in the way."

Brett considered all he had learned since leaving the railbus. "The free peoples."

Stan nodded. "It makes sense. Put these creatures out here to terrorize and decimate the free peoples, then sweep in and clear them out."

Jenna continued. "And start reclaiming the Wildlands." She looked at her compatriots working on the vehicles. "Plus, they know they can't hold their control much longer. The Roses are growing, along with other groups like ours around the world. Their hold on the people is loosening. That is why they have implemented more extreme measures like the 'rehabilitation' program your daughter was heading to, and other restrictions to keep you citizens under control."

Brett slumped to the ground. Suddenly, Olivia's voice called out, "Daddy, what is that?" They all turned. Jenna rushed over to Olivia, who was looking through a boarded-up window. Brett rushed to follow.

Jenna pulled Olivia to the side. "You need to be careful. We don't want to attract attention." Brett reached the window and peered out. Jenna looked out, too, and a smile adorned her face. In the middle of the street was a four-legged creature. It trotted forward a step as it sniffed the air. "That, sweetie, is a deer." Brett looked at the creature with wonder.

As he watched, something drew its attention, and it sprinted off. Brett heard the whirring sound of a craft and watched it enter the square where the deer had been standing. Brett pulled back from the boarded-up window, carefully peering out to watch the scene. As the craft landed, Jenna whispered, "Joe, we have company. It looks like a *scouter*."

Brett watched a hatch open on the door and two PPU officers emerge, along with three police bots. The officers remained by the craft, using comm devices, while the bots began scanning the area. Brett slunk back from the window as one bot approached their location. He looked up and saw the others holding their breath, Jenna holding Olivia tight.

A robotic voice ordered somebody to "Halt!" When Brett dared to peer out the window again, he saw it was pointing to someone out of view—the officers were now alerted. Suddenly, a form rushed in and crashed into it. The bot approaching the auto shop turned and began firing at the monstrous beast. Another beast slammed into one of the officers. Brett heard a snap as the beast tore the man in half. The other officer swiftly entered the craft and initiated the liftoff.

Brett was fully engrossed watching the scene when a third beast ran in and attacked the still-shooting bot closest to them. Following the collision, some shots went astray and struck the exiting craft. It crashed into a nearby building. The terrorlings ran toward the crash, leaving pieces of robot and the mutilated remains of the officer strewn about the square.

The sound of engines turning over drew Brett's attention. "Alright...let's load up," announced Joe. Brett took his family to the pickup and loaded them into the back. Jenna jumped in the cab next to Joe. The pilot, one soldier, Stan, and Debra filled the smaller vehicle. The last soldier, whom Brett heard called Sara, opened the garage door. After the sedan left the garage, she climbed into the back of the pickup with Brett and his family. The pickup followed the smaller vehicle.

They sped past the carnage in the square. A few twists and turns took them back to the main road. When they got there, Brett saw a group of monsters meandering up the street. As they breezed past the terrorlings, the creatures began hopping and screaming in excitement. The vehicle raced down the old roads of the Wildlands. The flock of monsters gave chase.

Brett pulled his family tight together.

Chapter Twenty-Six

CARNAGE

2163.05.25 | 13:02

Melissa was livid. They had the leader of the Gray Roses in custody, and he escaped. She looked around the wreckage of the transport. *Whose idea was it to transfer him via railbus?* Judging from the empty weapons cabinet, the survivors of the crash were well armed. Of course, if the incident at the Containment Facility hadn't occurred, he would have been taken there and become another "victim" of the doctor.

There were restrictions in place regarding air transport between Metros. Fuel was a big factor. She had filed the request. But somebody overstepped her and pushed for railbus transport.

She considered the passengers of the railbus. When she'd reached it, the only person left was the conductor and the dead guards. And *that* was a gruesome sight. Much like the guards at the facility, the conductor was torn to shreds, his guts strewn all over the vehicle. With the exception of the prisoner and his guards, the manifest was comprised of citizens. The guards had been killed by bolts from a firearm.

This was a mess.

Melissa exited the vehicle. They had seen the smoke about ten kilometers from where the railbus had stopped, just past the Susquehanna River. They determined the railbus was disabled by a low range EMP blast. When the scouter reported the wreckage here, Melissa left a small team to deal with the railbus while she and the rest of the crew reported to the crash site to investigate. As soon as she arrived, she found it empty. She ordered the scouter to inspect nearby locations where the survivors could be hiding out.

What puzzled her was the citizens. There were seven other passengers, including two young children. Going over the details of the passengers on her tablet, she considered each one. The husband and wife, the latter of which was being taken to the rehab facility, had nothing of note about them. Their son was in training and the woman had apparently lost her mind. Then there was the family. The girl was marked as having complications in her testing. What interested Melissa more was that the father worked at the same datacenter as Larson. Could there be a connection?

Finally, the solitary woman. The records were vague on her. Melissa had no doubts that she was a Gray Rose. Surveillance images were obscured, but even her blurry appearance was similar to the custodian at the Containment Facility.

Evans was carrying a case from their air cruiser as she approached. Several officers patrolled the area around the crash site. He pressed a button and legs unfolded as a stand for the case. He opened it and powered on the terminal. "Bad news!" he said. "We lost contact with the scouter. There was a mayday signal, but it cut out immediately. I'm deploying a drone now."

Evans pressed a button and slid a knob up in the drone terminal. The drone rose from the cruiser. He activated the camera and used the terminal to pilot the drone.

"What is the location of the mayday?" Melissa asked.

"An abandoned township called Elkton on the Wildland charts." As he piloted the drone, he flipped a switch to connect the terminal to the cruiser comms.

He pressed another button to play the mayday. "Bots destroyed! Officer Johnson is down. Attempting to evac. Shit! I'm hit. Going down! Mayday, mayday..."

Melissa took a breath. *Who shot down the scouter? The Roses?* She turned her attention to the monitor. A plume of smoke was visible in the wide-angle view. Evans piloted the drone closer. Melissa assessed the buildings would make a great hiding spot for the survivors from the transport.

When the drone reached an open area of the town, Evans switched to a narrow, close-up view. It was carnage. Pieces of the bots were strewn about the open area. The remains of Officer Johnson were like the remains of the conductor from the railbus, torn and shredded. Melissa found it disturbing that she was getting used to this. Evans said, "I don't believe that is the work of the Roses."

Melissa agreed. She watched as Evans turned the drone to inspect the area. Melissa noticed a building where a garage door had been left open. "They must have found old vehicles to use. Go to the scouter first. Check on the pilot." Evans guided the drone closer to the downed vehicle. "See if you can get a view inside the cockpit." Evans complied, bringing the drone in close and gliding it along the craft. As the cockpit came into view, so did the pilot. Glass was shattered all around, and the pilot was a bloody mess.

Melissa saw movement on the edge of the monitor. "What was that?" Evans turned the drone slowly. Looking directly into the camera, as if curious about the oddity before it, was one of the terrorlings. Though the face was a grotesque shell of what it had been before,

Melissa could see that it was human in origin. Pox marred its grayish skin. It tilted its head. Melissa was mesmerized by its human eyes.

Evans reversed the drone, but this seemed to agitate the creature. It growled and lunged forward. Suddenly, the view went crazy as the creature knocked the drone from the air. The connection went blank. Melissa stepped back. The thing was certainly hideous.

"We'll have to continue our pursuit of the fugitives from the air," she said.

She ordered the perimeter guards in, but stopped when she noticed one of them approaching the tree line. "What are you doing, Officer Blake?"

"There is somebody hiding in the trees. A girl." Melissa considered if it might be the girl from the railbus. Goose bumps rose on her arms. Officer Blake called out to the trees, "Come on out! There is no need to hide."

Melissa's instincts kicked in. "Stand down! Leave the girl alone!" It was too late. Officer Blake fell back as the "girl" leaped into the clearing and tackled him to the ground. She thrust her clawed hands under his helmet. It shot off like a bullet as the beast ripped his face apart. The thing stood up and let out a growl. She couldn't have been much older than fifteen or sixteen...when she was human.

Another officer fired his weapon at the creature. Bolts of energy struck her, but she did not slow. She charged the officer. Another officer aimed his weapon to fire but was cut off as another terrorling plowed into him from behind. Melissa looked around. More beasts were emerging from the trees.

Two approached her position when she felt arms grab her. Evans pulled her aside and shoved her toward the cruiser. "Go! Get out of here!" He ran toward the tree line, and the terrorlings followed him.

Melissa scrambled to the cockpit of the craft. She looked back to see Evans firing his gun at one beast as others piled on top of him.

She got the craft door open and entered. Something caught her foot. One of the beasts had dug its claws in as she entered the craft. Without hesitation, she drew her weapon and pointed it at the creature's face. She pulled the trigger and its head exploded. She shoved the body out with her wounded leg and pulled the hatch closed. Within moments, she was in the seat and taking off from the scene, abandoning her comrades to the carnage.

All thoughts of apprehending the fugitives were gone as she sped the craft toward the city. She had to report what had happened.

CHAPTER TWENTY-SEVEN

THE FINAL RUN

2163.05.25 | 13:26

The two antique vehicles gained momentum down the old road. Brett and Lindsey huddled with their children near the cabin of the truck. Sara, the soldier, remained at the rear of the truck bed, watching behind them with her gun at the ready. When they first hit the highway, the terrorlings were gaining on them. Sara had thrown something out at the horde and told them all to close their eyes. Brett pulled his kids close, but could not completely avoid the bright flash that lit up behind them. His eyes had mostly recovered, with only echoes of the light on the fringes of his sight.

The trick worked, it seemed, as he heard the cries of the beasts when the blazing light went off among them. Only one had made it past, and Sara was able to take it out with her rifle before it got too close. It was a comfort, at least, knowing that the creatures *could* die.

The road behind them was empty now, though Brett could still hear the howls and screams of the terrorlings.

The trees ominously hugged the road.

Occasionally they passed a building or two, mostly run down and vine covered. The vehicles slowed. Brett turned to look in the cab as

Jenna opened the sliding window between them. "Are you all okay back there?"

"Yes!" he replied. "Why are we slowing?"

"We have to make a turn. We can't take it too fast."

"Those things will catch up for sure." He looked back and could see them now, tirelessly running along the road at a distance behind them. Some were even using their hands in tandem with their feet.

Joe replied, "It can't be avoided. Otherwise, we will roll this vehicle and should any of us survive that, they'll catch up, anyway. Don't worry! This is our final run. We'll soon be at the school."

"I saw a drone from the school, so they should know that we are incoming now," added Jenna.

Joe shouted, "Be ready and hang on! We are about to make the turn." Brett heard tires squeal and dared to look forward as the car in front made its turn. "In three...two...one."

Brett held tight to his kids as the vehicle turned and slid to the side. Within moments, they were on the new street. He could hear noises in the growth along the roadside as the vehicle gained traction and momentum. A blood-curdling scream grabbed his attention, and he looked off to the side to see one beast leaping at the vehicle. Its clawed hand caught the truck bed. The creature glared hungrily at them as it attempted to control its grip on the speeding vehicle. Brett was so distracted that he didn't notice that others had emerged from the foliage close behind them, keeping pace with the vehicle.

A shot rang out as Sara blasted the clinging terrorling in the face. The energy bolt struck, and it lurched back, still clinging to the truck bed. It came forward, its face now half-ripped away, and gave a snarl. The children screamed and buried themselves in Brett's and Lindsey's arms. Brett could hear Lindsey crying. He also desired to, but fear paralyzed him.

Sara shot again. This time, the thing let go, falling and rolling into the oncoming creatures behind. A couple went down as the dead beast tripped them up, but quickly scrambled up and continued their pursuit. Sara turned her attention to them, firing shot after shot. They were barely phased despite the precision of her hits.

Brett heard a rustling and saw movement in the trees next to the vehicle. The shape of two creatures became apparent to him as they rapidly swung and passed from tree to tree, branch to branch. He looked down at the rifle beside him and pulled Olivia from him, guiding her to her mother. He took up the gun and inspected it. It wasn't like Sara's Magna rifle. It was an older type. Brett thought over the brief instructions given to him earlier on how to use it. He pulled the sliding lever to ready the weapon and moved to the back, next to Sara.

She glanced at him. "I don't have many shots left before my gun overheats." He nodded and pointed the gun toward the gaining creatures. "Place the butt of the rifle into your shoulder and lean into it when you take the shot," Sara instructed. He tried to follow the instructions. Looking down the sights, he picked a creature and pointed the rifle at it, then pulled the trigger. The kick nearly threw him back. The creature didn't even flinch.

He pointed again and squeezed the trigger. This shot struck the target in the shoulder, but it didn't slow down. Another terrorling finally went down as Sara's barrage ripped it apart. He heard the whine of her weapon as it started overheating. Brett took another shot with his rifle. The shot struck his target's foot, and it tripped. Even over the noise of the truck, he heard a loud crack as the thing's head struck the pavement.

"Good shot! Now give me your rifle and move back with your family. We are almost there, and I am trained with it."

Brett handed Sara the rifle and crawled back, satisfied that he'd done his bit.

Five of the beasts remained, chasing the vehicle, and one was getting close.

"Shit!" Joe cried. Brett felt the car slow slightly. A terrorling had managed to get onto the roof of the sedan, clawing at the top of the vehicle. The car swerved and careened off to the side, crashing into a tree. As the truck drove past, he could briefly see in the car—the pilot was slumped over, Debra was holding her head, and Stan looked terrified. Four of the terrorlings following broke away and ran straight to the crashed sedan. He could hear their screams fading behind as the monsters descended upon the vehicle.

Brett wanted to scream for them...to cry. He couldn't, as his focus shifted to the hulking shape in front of him. The remaining beast grabbed hold of the truck and pulled itself up. As Sara moved to shoot it, the creature retaliated, swiping at her with its claw. The force knocked the rifle out of her hands and sent it flying out of the truck, where it clattered on the pavement.

Brett sat there in terror as the beast turned its attention to him. It swiped at him, and he felt a sting as it slashed across his lower leg. The pain was searing, but it left his mind as the terrorling loomed over him. He thought it smiled as it dragged itself the rest of the way into the truck bed. It stood up and gave a victorious roar just as loud bangs rang in Brett's ears. He cringed from the pain of the noise, but when he looked up, he saw the beast was teetering at the rear. One more shot and the beast tumbled out of the back of the truck bed and rolled on the pavement behind.

Turning to the source of the shots, he expected to see Jenna shooting from that little window. Instead, he saw his beautiful wife, with Scotty clutched in one arm against her breast, Olivia clinging to her side, and her other arm extended with the handgun Joe had given her. Sara sat up, rubbing her arm, and nodded to his wife. Jenna smiled from the cab behind.

"She's a natural!" shouted Joe.

Again, he strained to hear Lindsey's response. "My dad taught me about guns when I was young." She seemed in a daze.

Joe's voice came again. "Son of a... Hold on!"

Brett craned around to look out the front windshield and saw another terrorling standing in front of them. Joe plowed the truck into it, sending the beast flying forward. The engine of the truck started to sputter, and the vehicle began to slow down. There was severe damage to the front carriage. The vehicle came to a stop and Joe and Jenna erupted from the cabin. "Let's go!" Joe yelled.

They scrambled out of the truck bed. Brett's leg nearly collapsed under him when he hit the pavement. He let out a scream. "Are you okay?" Lindsey asked.

"My leg! I nearly forgot that thing slashed it with its claw." He tried moving, but limped as he walked. "I'll be fine."

Joe was soon by their side. "We've got to move! Only a few more blocks until safety." Brett looked up the road and saw a makeshift fortress ahead. He could see people running around inside the fence.

"Come on!" Joe said as he put his arm around Brett to help him. "We're almost there."

They all began moving down the street as fast as they could. Brett winced with every step. He tried to put the pain out of his mind. He could see the gate to the fortress open. Relief washed over him. A group of people came out of the gate, some with guns.

"That's our escort party," said Joe.

The relief was short-lived. Screams rang out. They turned to see that the terrorlings were after them again, far back but closing fast.

Brett knew the escort would never reach them in time. He was slowing them down. He pulled himself from Joe's arm, taking the man's rifle as he did. "Go! There is no time. Get my family to safety."

Joe hesitated for a moment, then nodded. Lindsey screamed, "No!" He could hear the pain in her voice. He gave her an apologetic shrug. Sara took her by the arm, pulling her and Scott along toward the fortress.

"I love you!" he called to her. He could hear her cry as she was guided away.

"Daddy?" Olivia's voice rang in his ears. "What's going on?"

"You're going to safety, sweetheart."

He felt Jenna shove something into the pocket of his jacket. "Use this when the time comes. Find the ring and pull it out." She ran off ahead.

"Daddy!" Olivia cried as Joe scooped her up. "What do you want me to do?"

"Live!" Brett watched as Joe carried her off toward the fortress.

He turned and faced the terrorlings. They were getting close. With a quick glance to see the others closing the gap to the fortress, he armed the Magna rifle like he saw Sara do in the truck and pointed it at the closest creature. He fired it, striking the thing mid-torso. The kick of the rifle was not nearly as bad as the other one. The creature staggered. He fired again and again. Each shot seemed to have more of an effect than the previous. Finally, another shot took that one down. Three more to go.

They were close. He could see into their eyes. Human eyes. Their howls filled the night. He fired again. They were so close that the shots had more of an effect. He fired again. Another one went down, but still another leaped at him. He closed his eyes as it slammed into him.

Suddenly, he was on the ground. He could feel the heat of the beast's breath. He turned his head as it slashed at him, ripping him apart. The last creature joined the other one. The sensation in his legs was completely gone. He felt no pain.

With effort, he rotated his head to gaze towards the fortress. A smile stretched across his weary face. The escorts had met up with the others and were taking them in. A few soldiers were running toward him. A tug at his arm pulled his attention down. He realized his arm was no longer attached. It didn't matter. He had managed to slip his hand into his pocket. As the arm flew from his body, he glimpsed the ring dangling on his finger.

He closed his eyes. Thoughts of his family being safe rushed into his mind. He felt an immense heat erupt from his jacket pocket. Blackness overtook him.

EPILOGUE

2163.05.26 | 09:00

"**A**gent Davis, she will see you now!" Melissa turned to the speaker. The Executive Assistant was already back to her work on the terminal in front of her, barely regarding Melissa at all. She stood up and walked to the office door. Her limp slowed her down.

The door slid open, and Melissa stepped into the office. It was on the top floor of the building; the windows overlooked the Old Mall, where the Centennial had been celebrated just over a week ago. RP Morse stood by the window looking at the obelisk monument that stood in the Mall's center. Melissa moved to the center of the floor and waited for the President to address her.

Finally, RP Morse spoke. "It certainly is a fascinating structure, isn't it?

"Pardon, Madame President?"

The RP went on as if she didn't hear. "It has always fascinated me. Its simplicity in design and its magnitude astounds me. Perhaps that is why all the RPs before me allowed it to remain." She paused for a moment. "I just signed an order to tear it down. It is a relic of an old age. A new monument dedicated to the UGC will be erected in its place. It should have been taken down years ago."

Melissa didn't know how to respond. Finally, the RP turned and regarded her. The sternness in her face melted a little. "My dear! You have been through quite an ordeal. I have read your account of the situation. Your decision to disengage from pursuiting the fugitive has been noted and understood, given the circumstance. Your entire team?"

Melissa tensed at the mention of the incident and her team. She thought about her long-time partner, who sacrificed himself for her. "It was regrettable, but I saw no way to salvage them, and I needed to report what happened. Given my wounds, I was in no state to apprehend the fugitives."

The RP nodded. "Yes! With what you brought back, we can better prepare for a future operation. We know the region where the fugitives are holding up. Our old satellites show several areas that might act as their base, but we suspect decoys. Regardless, the technology of those ancient satellites is unreliable. I face a dilemma now."

Melissa considered the options that the UGC had in dealing with the threat. "The easiest answer would be to launch strikes to destroy the bases, but that would cause minimal impact. It is likely that they are already relocating. Any acts of retaliation against the Gray Roses would embolden their cells around the region."

"Very insightful!"

"There are reports of monsters in the city. Since the Containment Facility disaster two nights ago, three citizens have been found torn apart. And the rumors regarding the founding of the UGC, that its members artificially created the Plague, have been seeping into the city. It could cause dissidence among the citizens if we were to strike those sites."

RP Morse nodded. "Again, you have astute reasoning. Those rumors are troubling for us, indeed."

"You already have a plan. What will you do?"

She chuckled. "Nothing!" The answer struck Melissa like a brick. The RP gave another chuckle. She pressed a button on the desk, and a side door opened. Two UGC officers entered, flanking Dr. Weaver. Melissa's eyes opened wide.

Doctor Weaver grinned. "Hello, Agent Davis."

Melissa turned to the President, her look nearly demanding an explanation. She held her tongue, though.

"The doctor here has some use for us still. He has a device that will allow these creatures to be controlled. Care to explain, doctor?"

"Certainly. It is a collar that can be fastened to the neck of the terrorling. It sends jolts into the spinal cord that restricts the wearer. Using a remote device, we can change the creatures from a neutral state to docile or aggressive and back again. Working in conjunction with the restraints we use on prisoners to maneuver them, it can turn the creatures into effective shock troops for the UGC."

RP Morse stopped him. "It is all too technical for my taste. But the possibilities are endless. I am sending the good doctor here to New York Metro. They have over five hundred prisoners in their cells awaiting termination. He will assist the lab director at their research facility to turn the captives into these *terrorlings*. Many will be released into the Wildlands within the month. Others will be held to aid in strikes. We will begin taking back the Wildlands."

Melissa thought over the plan. "What about the ones loose in the city and the rumors going around?"

RP Morse snorted. "As for the latter, we will deny, of course. Lies and propaganda made up by the Gray Roses. We already have the message going out and I will address the matter tomorrow. I will also announce that the North American Region has been tasked with returning to space. We have several satellites ready to go, and our Division of Rocketry and Space is finalizing tests. We will see the first satellites launched in two weeks. They are state-of-the art and will give us a greater look at the Earth."

She locked eyes with Melissa. "As for the former, the monsters are no more than diseased terrorists that have made their way into the city. Fortunately, the disease is not spreadable, but can be very dangerous. We will put together a task force to hunt them down and eradicate the threat."

How the RP continued to stare at Melissa made her realize something. "You want me to lead the task force."

RP Morse smiled. "You understand."

Melissa stiffened. "I'll begin putting together a new team immediately. I already have some ideas about who will be perfect for the job."

"Good! Containing the threat in the city is of utmost importance. Meanwhile, the doctor will assist his director in manufacturing his terrorling recipe. We will disperse them to other Metros here in the North American Region first. The terrorlings will do their job of eradicating the terrorists. Then we will sweep in and reclaim the Wildlands." RP Morse turned to the guards. "Prepare the doctor for immediate transfer."

She looked at Melissa and smiled. "Go and see about your tasks. Everything will sort itself out." Melissa didn't know why, but the RP's smile unsettled her. She nodded and left the office of the Regional President.

***

The grounds of the old university were bustling with activity. People ran around frantically as they prepared to abandon the site. A small part of Jenna was sad about that. She had learned that her great-grandfather had graduated from that school with honors. She didn't really know much about him, but it created a small sentimental connection to the school. Still, she knew they could no longer stay there. The UGC would likely close in on the school in a matter of weeks, if not days.

As she walked the grounds, she came upon the family, Lindsey and her two children. They were settling into the group nicely; especially given everything they were going through. She volunteered to head out with them as they left for the new site. They would need somebody to look after them. Of course, she wasn't the only one going with them. She saw Sara nearby, loading up the vehicle with supplies.

Jenna left the gates and walked down the road. The area around the school was deemed secure, and guards patrolled it as vehicles left to begin their pilgrimage to various outposts up and down the coast. The decision was made quickly. Salvage teams went out to recover the remains of those lost within sight of the school. The citizen, Brett Hardin, along with Jack, Mark, and the couple. Miraculously, the woman was found alive and being treated. Her husband, Stan, had covered her as the beasts ripped him apart. She was found under his remains, wedged on the rear floorboard of the sedan. Despite his gruffness towards her, he truly loved her to the end.

She approached the location where Brett Hardin made his final stand. Ahead of her, she could make out another person, fixated on the same spot. She stepped up beside Joe. Without turning to face him, her eyes locked on the small crater. "I don't know if I could have done it."

Joe stared at the spot. "You'd be surprised what you could do when pressed. For him, it was worth the price." He turned to look at her. "If it was Kara, you would have. And she would do the same for you." She winced a bit at the mention of her sister's name. He put his hand on her shoulder. "I was sorry to hear about her."

"She did what she had to do." She turned to him. "Is that why you got captured? I wouldn't have thought that you could have been taken so easily."

He didn't immediately respond. "Even the greatest have their bad days."

"It wouldn't have mattered. You would have been too late, and likely would have ended like her." She looked back at the crater. "We are grateful to him. I didn't know what to think when I first saw him on that platform. I guess I just saw another UGC stooge. But the more I spoke with him, the more I understood he was just washed. I could see him shifting throughout our journey here."

"He was just trying to survive. Can you blame him?"

She shook her head. "No! I used to pity the citizens. But getting to know him during that brief time, I sympathize. Perhaps, one day, when all of this is over, they will erect a statue of him on this spot. He may have changed the course of the future."

A fresh voice entered the conversation. "Yes! We have something that we haven't had before. Hope! We already started disseminating the information that we gained. The data was very thorough."

Jenna looked at Rachel as she joined them. "I am glad that something good can come from the data I extracted."

Rachel smiled. "The information is making the circuits and reaching the citizens. Our cells around the world are disseminating it as well. Oh, I am sure that the UGC will counter it in some fashion. But the truth is out there. Eventually, the people will accept it for what it is."

"What of the family?"

"A fine family indeed. Especially the girl. I can sense something about her. With my guidance, she will be of great importance. This war is just beginning, and it will be a long one. We will need her, and others like her, if we are to have a chance of succeeding."

They all stood there in silence for a few moments longer. Finally, Rachel spoke up again. "Come, let us finish preparations. The road ahead will be long and hard. Until now, our successes have been minor. Soon, the real fight will begin."

Acknowledgments

Editing

Blue Pen Books- Victoria Griffin (*Owner*), Anjanette Barr (*Book Boss*), Kerry Stapley (*Developmental Editor*), and Chelsea Cambeis (*Line Editor*)

Illustrations and Art

Rebeccacovers (cover art) and BMR Williams (*Maps*)

BETA Readers

Glenda C, Robbie Seal, Robert Young, Norma Garcia, and Shannon Casey

Other Support

Lexy Layman, Savannah Serio, Sophia Serio, Salvatore C Serio, Jr., Joan M. McGrady, Vickie Kohlhepp, Robert Young, Angela M. Horst

Thank you to all my friends and family who supported and encouraged me throughout the production of this novel.

ABOUT AUTHOR

S. J. Serio was born in Baltimore, MD where he currently lives with his family. He has served in the U.S. Navy and worked in many jobs of different fields including information technology, transportation services, and hospital services. He decided to pursuit his love of writing and creativity and is the founder of Infinite Worlds, LLC.

www.ingramcontent.com/pod-product-compliance
Lightning Source LLC
Chambersburg PA
CBHW072124300726
48975CB00003B/914

Gershwin's Last Waltz

and Other Stories

Gershwin's Last Waltz

and Other Stories

FRANK FROST

ARPress
45 Dan Road Suite 5
Canton MA 02021

Hotline:1(888) 821-0229
Fax:1(508) 545-7580

Ordering Information:
Quantity sales. Special discounts are available on quantity purchases by corporations, associations, and others. For details, contact the publisher at the address above.

Printed in the United States of America.

ISBN-13:	Paperback	979-8-89330-552-4
	eBook	979-8-89330-553-1

Library of Congress Control Number: 2024900777